SURRENDER'S EDGE

SURRENDER'S EDGE

...The kiss slowed, losing that desperate edge, and Nash put his hands on Geoffrey's hips, pulling him closer. Geoffrey could taste the sweet fruit juice on Nash's lips, and something else, something a bit bitter. He knew it was Sunny. He knew she could be coming to look for them at any minute, and knew what he was doing was wrong. So wrong. But desire flooded his body and he couldn't make himself stop. He was dying for it, dying for the attention, dying to explore every bit of Nash's mouth, and then further, to know every inch of his body.

"You've been wanting to do that for awhile," Nash murmured when Geoffrey finally lifted his head, but he didn't step away.

"Yeah, awhile," Geoffrey agreed.

"Why didn't you?"

Geoffrey's eyes widened. "Why didn't I slam you against a wall and kiss you? Did I have any reason to think you'd welcome that sort of treatment?"

"You really are oblivious, aren't you?" Nash asked, but not unkindly.

"Who said I was oblivious?"

"Me," Sunny said from behind him.

Geoffrey stiffened, taking a halting step backward. He didn't want to turn to face her. How could he explain pushing her boyfriend against the tree and devouring his mouth? He looked at Nash helplessly, but Nash didn't seem concerned at all.

In fact, he was smiling...

SURRENDER'S EDGE

BY

PEPPER ESPINOZA

AMBER QUILL PRESS, LLC
http://www.amberquill.com

SURRENDER'S EDGE
AN AMBER QUILL PRESS BOOK

Amber Quill Press, LLC
http://www.amberquill.com
http://www.amberheat.com

Layout and Formatting provided by: ElementalAlchemy.com

PUBLISHED IN THE UNITED STATES OF AMERICA

*I would like to dedicate this book to Sigrid and Kim
for all of their encouragement and inspiration.
Thank you, ladies.*

CHAPTER 1

Of course they were sleeping together. Of course it had only been a matter of time. He walked into the room and her eyes sparkled. She was all he could talk about after work. So it didn't come as a surprise to Geoffrey when he finally saw the indisputable evidence with his own eyes. Saw, heard it, smelled it even. He only witnessed the two of them for a second, but it was a second that would stretch to an infinity and sear itself to his brain.

Geoffrey's chest hurt. His head hurt. He returned to his desk dazed, unable to see anything except them, together. Sunny on Nash's lap, his hands up her blouse, her mouth on his neck. Jealousy was a poison-tipped arrow in his heart. Of course they were sleeping together.

He sat down heavily in his chair, his eyes drawn to the desk on the opposite side of the room. Sunny sat there every day, her eyes bright, her smile wide. She flirted with him, flirted with their clients, flirted with Nash. It hadn't meant anything. Geoffrey knew she never meant it when she batted her eyes at him. But how was he supposed to know she meant it when she looked at Nash?

The phone rang. He knew he should answer it. He let it ring. After six rings, the voicemail picked up and the small office was plunged into silence again. Geoffrey waited for any signs from Nash's office, but there was nothing. Perhaps the two of them were so wrapped up in each other that they hadn't heard the phone ring at all.

Geoffrey leaned forward, resting his head on his desk, his arms cushioning his brow. He took several deep breaths, willing his stomach

1

to settle. Every time he closed his eyes, he saw them. Saw them together, but the image evolved. Sunny wasn't just kissing his neck, she was trailing her mouth down his chest, unbuckling his belt, wrapping her lips around his cock. And Nash wasn't just groping her under her blouse. She was naked, her nipples hard, her flesh hungry for his touch.

Geoff groaned. He was going to torture himself with these visions for the rest of his life. He'd never stop. He'd poke and prod at the memory until it was flaring in agony like an abscessed tooth.

The unmistakable sound of Nash's door opening in the silent office jerked Geoffrey from his thoughts. He straightened quickly, wiping his face of any emotion as Sunny stepped out of the room. Her shirt was straight, her hair combed, and her lipstick reapplied, but now he could see it all over her. How had he missed it before? The flush of her cheek, the light in her eye, the playful smile that tugged on her full lips.

"Hey, slugger. Sorry I missed the phone. The boss man wanted me to take some notes."

Geoff stared at her. How many times had she lied like that before? How many times had he completely ignored it?

"I missed it, too," he said, his voice bland. "You'll have to check the messages."

"No problem. Hey, Geoff?"

"Yeah?" Geoff busied himself with the computer, opening random files, hoping she would get the hint.

"Can you give me a lift tomorrow afternoon? I need to go to the dentist, and they told me I can't drive myself home."

Geoffrey's gaze darted from the computer screen, to her, and back to the computer. "I'm sorry, I'm busy."

"You're busy? Geoffrey, I schedule all your appointments. You have tomorrow open, or else I wouldn't have asked," she pointed out.

"I'm busy," Geoffrey repeated. He forced the next words out of his mouth. "Maybe Nash can help you?"

"Nash has a meeting tomorrow," Sunny countered. "He's meeting with the Bowies. Your biggest clients. Ring any bells?"

"Oh. Right. Can you take a cab?"

Sunny's face fell, and Geoffrey hated himself for it. She didn't look upset, just disappointed. And confused. And why wouldn't she be? Geoffrey had always bent over backward to help her, agreeing to a variety of favors, from acting as chauffeur to fixing her garbage disposal one memorable Thanksgiving afternoon.

In other words, he had never told her no.

2

Until now.

And he couldn't even stand to look at her.

"I guess I could."

"Look, Sunny, I'm sorry, it's just…"

She held up her hand. "No, no, I understand. Hey, it's not like you're my errand boy, right?"

I'm not your anything, Geoffrey thought before turning back to the computer. He didn't look at her, but he was all too aware of her presence. He was always too aware of Sunny's presence. And he thought, maybe, one day she wouldn't see him as her best girlfriend who happened to have a reliable car.

The words in front of him were meaningless. He wasn't going to get any work done, and there were still four more hours before he could realistically go home.

Nash's door opened again. Geoffrey didn't look away from the computer until he heard his name.

"Hey, Geoff. Do you have the Fielding file?"

Geoffrey silently reached for the thick folder on his desk and handed it to Nash. He couldn't lift his gaze to meet Nash's eyes, and was careful not to let their fingers brush. He didn't feel the same sort of despair over Nash that he felt for Sunny—that ship had sailed years ago and he'd learned to live with it. But it still hurt. A little. In a secret place that Geoffrey didn't like to acknowledge.

"You okay, Geoff? You look a little pale."

Geoffrey glanced up, forcing a smile. "I'm fine."

"Good." Nash turned back to his office, sparing a brief smile Sunny's direction before disappearing behind the door.

"You do look a little pale," Sunny observed.

"Maybe I just need some air. I think I'll take lunch now."

Sunny frowned, confused. "Take lunch? Didn't you *just* get back from lunch? I thought you left just after twelve."

"No, I…" Geoffrey stopped, understanding. When he had slipped out to get the papers he'd left in his car, she'd assumed he was going to lunch. So she had taken her own break on Nash's lap. "I got caught up in traffic. I came back before I had a chance to eat."

Now she looked at him sympathetically. "Man, I hate it when that happens. That's why I started eating here at the office. No wonder you look a bit green around the gills. Why don't you go around the corner to the deli? Get yourself a sandwich?"

The hell of it was, Geoffrey could actually see that she cared. She was concerned about him. She didn't want him to be pale, or green around the gills, or miserable. Geoffrey understood at that moment that if he stayed, if he had to see the two of them together—and pretending they weren't together—it would make him crazy.

"Thanks, Sunny. I think I'll do that."

She beamed at him. "Hey, I need you to be in a good mood. When you're not happy, the whole office falls apart."

Geoffrey snorted. "I'm sure my empty stomach isn't that dire." The pain in his chest, however, was something else entirely. "Do I have any appointments this afternoon?"

She consulted her calendar, biting the tip of her pen. "Jack Henderson is going to be here at three, but I think that can be rescheduled," she said helpfully.

"Could you do that for me?" Geoffrey asked. "I'd really appreciate it."

He hated to let his emotional turmoil affect his job, but he couldn't even breathe with her in the room. He just needed an afternoon. A little time. A little space. He needed to let himself become accustomed to the new shape of things. Nash and Sunny wouldn't keep their relationship from him forever. When they finally decided to stop lying to him and come clean, he would need to be prepared.

And that might take a little time.

"Yeah, no problem, Geoff. Should I tell Nash you're taking the afternoon off?"

Geoffrey knew Nash deserved to be told personally, but he didn't want to talk to him. Not until he could look at the other man without losing his composure. "Yeah. Thanks."

"Maybe it's some sort of bug?" she suggested.

Geoffrey stood, pulling on his jacket. "Maybe."

"Promise me that if it gets worse, you'll go see a doctor?"

"If what gets worse?" Geoffrey asked, opening his briefcase and loading it with papers.

"Whatever is wrong with you. I mean, last winter you had the stomach flu and you dragged yourself to work. It must be pretty serious if you're taking some time off," she observed.

Geoffrey looked up, finally meeting her eyes. "Yeah, I think it might be."

"Maybe I'll bring some chicken soup for you later on."

"Thanks," Geoffrey said softly. "But that's not necessary."

"You'd do the same for me."

He would do the same for her. He'd do anything for her, if she asked him. He'd be anything she wanted. "Call me if there's an emergency. I'll keep my cell phone on."

"Yes, sir."

Geoffrey paused at the door, turning to look over his shoulder once more. Sunny was typing, her manicured fingers flying over the keys. Over her shoulder, he saw Nash through the office window, bent over his desk, his brow furrowed in thought. His heart skipped a beat.

Of course they were sleeping together.

*   *   *

Geoffrey stretched out on the couch, a beer in one hand, his phone in the other. After some consideration, he decided to turn it off. There might be an emergency at the office, but he doubted anything would happen that Nash couldn't handle himself. And it technically wasn't his responsibility either.

It was all Nash. Nash had had the original idea to start their own firm. Nash had had the big dream in the corner of their first basement office. Nash had had the goals, the foresight, and even the money. Nash had always seemed too big for his small life, and that meant success was a given. Fate. Nobody as driven, as clever as Nash could remain in a dingy basement office.

Geoffrey had been caught up in his wake. He'd followed Nash from their first small-time job at Brown and White, agreeing to invest what little money he had into Nash's dream. He had then followed Nash from office to office, job to job, client to client, happy to do everything in his power to build Nash's dream.

He still remembered the day they hired Sunny. It was the week after they moved into their most recent office space. They had felt invincible that week. And why not? They had a roster of clients that rivaled consulting firms twice their size, and Geoffrey had managed to secure a prime location for their permanent office.

If Geoffrey was ever going to have the courage to reveal his feelings for Nash, it would have been then, in that golden time, when everything was going their way. But in the end, Geoffrey had changed his mind, unable to risk the good relationship they did have. They were partners. They had a business together. If Geoffrey made a pass and Nash rejected him, they would still be business partners.

Like they were still business partners now.

Geoff supposed his feelings for Sunny might have been misplaced.

Perhaps he was looking for something to refocus his emotions on, looking for a distraction from Nash, and his eyes had fallen on her. Or maybe she was just one of the most gorgeous, surprising, exhilarating women he'd ever met.

Either way, it made sense that the two people he loved more than anything would be together. Women never even spared a second glance at Geoffrey when Nash was in the room. Geoff knew he wasn't ugly. Some days he thought he might even be handsome. But Nash was something else entirely. He was ridiculously handsome, to the point of being beautiful, his face and body something out of ancient Greece. And he had the easiest smile that lit his face.

But Geoffrey knew Sunny would never be able to see him. Not while Nash blinded her.

Why had they hid it? Why not just tell him? Maybe he didn't need a formal announcement, but Nash was supposed to be his best friend. Didn't best friends tell each other when they were banging the receptionist? Unless Nash knew about his feelings for Sunny, or Sunny had somehow managed to figure out his feelings for Nash.

Geoffrey pinched the bridge of his nose. It was too complicated. He'd created a mess, albeit unknowingly. He hadn't meant to fall in love with two people. He didn't even know it was possible to be in love with two people at once.

He couldn't see them again. Not like this. It hurt. He knew he never had a chance with either one of them, knew they saw other people, knew Nash in particular had a long list of willing partners, but that was different. He didn't know how or why, but it was completely different.

Why didn't they just tell him? Why did he have to learn it this way? Why couldn't he just get over it?

He downed the beer in greedy gulps, hoping the alcohol would mute the questions. It didn't seem to make a difference at all, so he tried again with a second beer. And then a third. And a fourth. And then he lost count.

Geoffrey had never been much of a drinker, but something had to wash the memory from his mind. Something had to smother the pain in his gut. But it didn't work.

At one point, when his living room was plunged into complete darkness because the sun had disappeared and he couldn't be bothered to turn on the light, he imagined the two of them in Nash's bed.

He couldn't do this.

CHAPTER 2

"Geoffrey, I'm going to need you to look over the notes for the Bowie meeting. I've been over them and over them, and the numbers just aren't making sense. I know you said it'd be fine, but I..." Nash stopped short, staring at Geoffrey's empty desk. "Where's Geoff?"

Sunny shook her head. "He didn't come in at all, he didn't call, and when I tried to call him, he didn't pick up."

Nash frowned. "Geoffrey, *our* Geoffrey hasn't called and can't be reached and you didn't tell me?"

"I just found out," Sunny said defensively. "I was going to tell you right now."

Nash rubbed the back of his neck, the file in his hand forgotten. He had known Geoff for over ten years, and the other man never took a day off. Not voluntarily. Nash had resorted to bodily hauling him out of the office a few times when he was too sick to sit up, and the time his grandmother died Nash had to lock him out completely, but other than that? And to not call?

He grabbed his coat and his keys without hesitating. "Sunny, you're going to have to hold down the fort while I'm gone. I need to make sure he's all right."

"Of course."

"He didn't say anything to you yesterday, did he?" Nash asked.

"No. I mean, he seemed a little out of it after lunch, but..."

Nash paused on his way to the door to kiss her, and she responded like she always did—immediately, willingly. "Call me if you hear from

7

him first."

"Call me when you find him," Sunny countered. "So I can stop worrying."

"Promise," Nash said with a small smile before ducking out the door.

He drove directly to Geoffrey's small townhouse, cursing each red light that stood between him and his goal. He couldn't help but think of the worst-case scenarios, and each one made his heart pinch. But it was impossible to remain optimistic. Geoffrey didn't just disappear like that. Geoff was fundamentally incapable of being thoughtless.

Nash parked on the street and hurried up the familiar walk. Geoffrey had been living there as long as Nash knew him, and at this point, Nash couldn't imagine the other man living anywhere else. Geoff had mentioned buying a new house when their firm began to take off, but that never seemed like a genuine interest. Now Nash stood outside the door, knocking with increasing desperation.

After five minutes of no response, he fished his key ring out and found the spare that belonged to Geoff. He turned the lock and paused a second to brace himself for what he might find. If he was lucky, the worst thing to greet him would be the empty home—though then he'd have to start scouring the city to find his friend.

"Geoffrey?" Nash called as he stepped into the living room. "You here?"

The first thing that struck Nash was the smell. Alcohol hung like a cloud in the air, and beneath that, the bitter scent of vomit. All the shades were pulled and the lights off, but even in the dim light, Nash could see the empty beer bottles strewn across the floor, stacked haphazardly on the table, and balanced perilously on the arm of the couch. He didn't even know Geoffrey liked to drink.

"Geoff?" He moved out of the empty living room to the hallway. A quick glance into the bedroom confirmed that Geoffrey wasn't hiding there. He turned to the bathroom, and after a few steps heard the unmistakable sound of puking. The sort of puking only drunks and sick children indulged in.

Nash knocked on the closed bathroom door lightly. "Geoffrey? Are you okay?"

"Go away." Muffled and weak.

"You a bit hungover?"

"A bit. Please…"

"It's not like you to drink in the middle of the week," Nash said, though he was still more concerned than angry. "Or at all."

Geoffrey's only response was a groan.

"I'm going to break the door down if you don't open it," Nash called, but his tone was far from threatening.

"That's not necessary, Nash." Even in his sickened and hungover state, Geoffrey's exasperation was clear. "The damned thing is open."

Nash turned the knob and pushed the door open. "Oh," he said, smiling sheepishly.

Geoffrey looked at him with unreadable, bloodshot eyes for a moment, then turned back to the toilet. He looked like shit. Nash had never seen him look so awful. His face was pasty-white and slick with sweat, and he was still wearing his clothes from the day before. The shirt was half-unbuttoned and untucked, his pants unzipped, and he really stank.

"What the fuck happened to you?" Nash demanded.

"Nothing," Geoffrey muttered. His body heaved, but he caught himself, and sunk back against the wall. "Nothing. Didn't I tell you to go away?"

"How much did you have to drink last night?"

"I don't know. How many bottles are out there?"

"You don't keep that much beer on hand," Nash said, confused.

"Clearly I bought more."

"Why?"

Geoffrey looked at him like he couldn't believe the extent of Nash's stupidity. "Because I felt like drinking."

Nash sighed. "Yes, I understand that. But I've never known you to drink like that."

"There might be a lot of things you don't know about me," Geoffrey said, and now he sounded tired. Resigned.

"Geoffrey, what's going on?"

Geoff pushed himself to his feet. Or tried to. After several shaky attempts, he was standing, eyes level with Nash's. "Nothing, I'm fine."

Nash grabbed him by the upper arms, but resisted the urge to shake him like a doll. He didn't have the most even temper, and now Geoffrey was tap-dancing on his last nerve, despite his very real concern.

"You are not fine. Goddamnit, Geoff, just tell me what the fuck is going on. I have a big meeting in just a few hours, and I needed your help with the numbers, and now I find you here, and you probably can't even remember your own *phone* number, and what the hell are we going to do?"

"555-2298," Geoffrey rattled off.

"Geoff…"

Geoffrey pulled away from him and stumbled backward, his head connecting with the wall. He didn't seem to notice though. "The Bowie numbers? Sorry, Nash, I can't help you."

"Why can't you help me? *You* put the proposal together!"

Geoffrey nodded. "I can help you, but I'm not going to."

Nash opened and closed his mouth like a wounded fish. What the fuck was going on around here? Just yesterday, Geoffrey had been his normal, bright, efficient, *normal* self. Now this drunk was standing in front of him and telling him he wasn't going to help, and what the fuck was going on?

"You're not going to?" Nash asked, his voice betraying his shock. "You're not going to help me with the numbers? Why not? Do you have a headache?"

"Actually, yes, I do have a headache. A very serious one. But that's not why I'm not going to help."

"Then what's the reason?"

"I quit."

Nash blinked. "What?"

"I quit," Geoff repeated calmly.

"You quit. You quit? You can't fucking quit, Geoffrey! You own half the fucking business!" Geoffrey winced at Nash's exclamation, but Nash didn't care. "Why? Why are you doing this?"

"You can buy me out, Nash. I would just give you my half, but I do have to keep a roof over my head."

"Buy you out?" Nash repeated, as if the words were meaningless. In a way, they were meaningless. Because Nash was not going to buy Geoffrey out, and he was not going to let him quit. "I can't."

"I assure you, it's quite easy. I'll have my lawyer draw something up this week."

Nash stared at him. There was no way in hell they were having this conversation. It just wasn't happening. They were *partners*. It didn't work without Geoffrey. That was the whole fucking *point* of having Geoffrey around. Nothing was right without him.

"No. No, you're not thinking clearly, Geoff. Whatever happened last night…whatever is happening now, you aren't thinking clearly."

Geoffrey looked at him with suddenly serious and sober eyes. "No, Nash, I am thinking quite clearly. I promise you. I know exactly what

I'm doing."

Nash put his hand on Geoffrey's shoulder again, but this time he pulled away immediately. "Why don't you get some rest? We can discuss this more tomorrow somewhere that smells less like vomit."

Geoffrey looked like he was going to protest, but he nodded after a moment and followed Nash out of the bathroom.

"I trust you can show yourself out," Geoff said quietly.

"Do you want me to get you anything? Something for your head?" Nash offered.

"I'm fine," Geoff repeated. "Go. I'm sure Sunny is wondering what's keeping you."

"Yeah...wait, what?"

"What?"

"What did you mean about Sunny?" Nash asked.

Geoffrey shook his head. "Nothing. I meant I'm sure you need to get back to work."

"Sunny was really worried about you this morning. Why didn't you at least call?" Nash asked.

"Well, now you can tell her I'm just fine," Geoffrey said, pushing him to the door.

"You're not fine. Damn it, Geoffrey. I've never seen you this not fine before. Look, please, as your friend, I'm asking, what's wrong?"

Geoffrey paused, regarding him with his unsettlingly clear eyes. "We are friends, Nash. Best friends, wouldn't you say?"

"Well, yeah. I mean, you know me better than anybody else, Geoff."

"And would you say that best friends do usually share important news, and sometimes even big secrets? Things like new relationships?"

"Of course, Geoff. Is this what you're upset about? Did somebody break..." Nash paused, his eyes widening. "Things like new relationships?"

"Yeah, things like that."

"Oh, my God, Geoffrey. How did you know?"

"I saw the two of you yesterday," Geoffrey admitted, and now he was looking at everything except Nash. "In your office."

"Is that why you're..." He gestured at the empty bottles. "I mean, Geoffrey, why didn't you just talk to me about it?"

"Get out, Nash."

"But Geoffrey..."

"Just get out. Please."

Nash nodded, understanding that they weren't going to get any further in this discussion. "I can show myself out."

"Please do."

It was almost a relief to step out of the dark house and into the sunshine, but a part of Nash was still with Geoffrey. He couldn't even be surprised by Geoffrey's reaction to his relationship with Sunny. Hadn't they decided to keep it a secret because they knew on some level it would hurt him? But even Nash hadn't been prepared for the extent of Geoffrey's pain.

He was surprised, and a little confused. He knew Geoffrey had shown a small interest in Sunny, but he seemed content enough to keep their relationship on a purely professional level, with occasional forays into easy friendship. He had never made a pass at Sunny, never asked her out, never indicated that he wanted anything more out of their relationship.

And Nash knew that Sunny had been waiting for a sign. Any sign. Had been waiting for over a year for Geoffrey to make even the slightest effort, but he never did.

So now he was locking himself away, and drinking in the dark, and *quitting* on the business that they had built from the ground up with nothing but sweat and blood?

A part of Nash wanted to turn on his heel, march right back into the house, and beat some sense into Geoffrey. But that wouldn't accomplish anything. It wouldn't even make Nash feel better. With a final glance over his shoulder, he walked back to his car. He wasn't going to let Geoffrey get away with this. He didn't know how to stop him, but they had worked too hard for too long to let a girl—even a girl as great as Sunny—come between them now.

*　　*　　*

Sunny looked about as shocked and upset as Nash felt. "He what?"

"Got drunk and got sick."

"Geoffrey? Geoffrey Kirk got *drunk* and spent the morning puking?" Sunny asked.

"That's the guy, yes." Nash leaned against Geoffrey's desk, fidgeting with the name plaque. It would always be Geoffrey's desk. He didn't care what Geoffrey said.

"Why?"

Nash knew that simple question was coming. Had, in fact, spent the entire drive to the office trying to think of an answer. The truth was always handy, but he didn't know if it was appropriate. It seemed vitally important to protect his friend's privacy, but at the same time, Geoffrey's decision to leave affected Sunny, too, and she deserved to have all the information.

"He saw us together yesterday."

"Oh," Sunny breathed.

"Yeah. And I guess he was a little upset."

"You guess he was a little upset?" Sunny shook her head. "He was probably really crushed, Nash. I told you we shouldn't try to keep it from him."

"But you knew it would hurt him if he knew the truth?" Nash asked.

"Well, yeah. I mean, he clearly has a thing for you. Probably always has."

Nash held up his hands, shocked. "What? A thing for *me*? Are you out of your mind?"

Sunny cocked her brow. "Nash, are you blind? He dotes on you. I wasn't sure at first, of course. But when I kept sending him very blatant signals and he kept ignoring them, I figured he must have eyes for somebody else."

"And that somebody else is me?"

"Yeah."

Nash shook his head. "You're crazy. Geoffrey's never had eyes for me. We're just friends. Besides, I don't even think Geoff...swings that way. I mean, it's not like I've ever seen him dating a guy, and I've known him for a long time."

"Do you?" Sunny asked.

"Do I what?"

"Swing that way? Have you ever dated a guy?"

"A few times. In college," Nash mumbled.

"Oh."

"Is that a problem?"

"Hey, all I'm saying is that maybe he never said anything because he thought *you* didn't swing that way," Sunny explained.

Nash shook his head. "It doesn't matter. It wasn't me he wanted, it was you."

"Me? Did you miss the part where I sent very loud, very obvious signals?" Sunny asked.

"No, I did not. I noticed what you were doing, even if he didn't. Geoffrey can be a bit...oblivious."

Sunny sighed. "So what you're telling me is that even though you thought Geoff had a thing for me, you asked me out anyway. And even though I thought Geoff had a thing for you, I accepted anyway. And then we began carrying out an affair behind his back because we both knew that if he found out, he'd be upset. And now he has found out, and he is upset."

"And he wants to quit."

Now Sunny gaped at him. "Quit? Geoff can't quit!"

"That's what I told him. He said he wants me to buy him out and he'll contact his lawyer in the morning," Nash explained.

"We're the worse people ever."

"I know."

"We can't let him go, Nash."

"I know." Nash studied his shoes, his mind spinning. He needed to fix this. He needed to fix all of it. "Do you have feelings for Geoffrey?"

"Nash, I...I mean, I'm with you now, right?"

He looked up, meeting her eyes calmly. "I'm not going to get mad, Sunny. Do you?"

"Maybe," she admitted, and now she couldn't look at him. "A little. I mean, Geoff is a great guy. Even if he is a bit emotionally unavailable. Do you?"

"Have feelings for Geoff? I...he's my best friend."

"But do you want it to be more than that?" Sunny pressed.

"I thought about it. Once or twice."

"I think we can fix this."

Nash closed the space between them, taking her arm. "I don't want to give you up, Sunny. I don't want to lose Geoffrey, but I don't want to lose you either."

"No, I don't want that," Sunny assured him. "But maybe Geoffrey wants both of us?"

"You mean, instead of it just being you and me...it'll be the three of us?"

"Right. If you think you're up to it."

Nash nodded. It sounded insane, but on the other hand, it sounded like it could work. He'd be willing to try anything if it meant Geoffrey wouldn't leave. "I think it might be worth a shot."

Sunny curled her fingers around his tie and pulled him close. "You go to your meeting now, boss man, and I'll do what I do best."

"What's that?" Nash asked, his lips brushing against hers.

"Save your ass."

CHAPTER 3

The first thing Geoffrey became aware of when he emerged from the pain of the hangover was shame. Deep, deep shame. He only had a vague memory of what happened that morning, but he remembered enough to know that he had been a real prick. Puking his guts out in front of Nash, and then quitting.

He had actually said the words *I quit*. He'd never intended to. But he'd opened his mouth, and the words spilled from his lips, and he couldn't call them back. Even when Nash gave him a chance, he couldn't take them back. And he'd never intended to get so drunk he couldn't see straight. And he certainly had never intended to have that scene with Nash.

Now he didn't know how to fix it. Or if it should even be fixed. He had been out of line. He had been wrong to leave the office yesterday, wrong to get drunk, wrong to tell Nash he quit. Wrong to care at all. Nash and Sunny were adults, and what they did in their private lives was none of his concern or business.

Geoffrey cleaned his living room and kitchen mechanically, gathering all the bottles and disposing of them. The house still smelled, though. He vacuumed the carpet, scrubbed and mopped the kitchen, and even dusted. But it didn't look right and he didn't feel better.

He knew he should call Nash, but didn't know what he should say. Tell him that he didn't mean it? That he didn't want to sell his part of the business? God, how could he even explain his erratic behavior?

Geoffrey turned his cell phone on, staring at the list of missed calls.

Most of them were from Sunny, but a few came from Nash. He scrolled through the list, trying to figure out what he'd say. *Hey, Nash. Sorry I was such a jerk. I didn't mean any of it. How did the Bowie meeting go? Do you still need me to look at those numbers?*

Maybe he wouldn't have to call and explain at all. Maybe he could just show up at the office the next morning, cleanly shaven and smiling. Perhaps with an offering of some kind. Nash liked bagels, Sunny liked donuts, they both enjoyed Danishes.

Or maybe he had just isolated his only friends in a childish fit of jealousy.

Maybe they'll understand.

But how could they understand when he didn't understand it himself? Nash hadn't taken anything from him. Sunny was never his, never going to be his. And as for Nash himself, he had already come to terms with it. Wasn't it enough that they were happy? Shouldn't he just be happy for them?

Geoffrey dialed the first four digits of Nash's number, then hesitated. But Nash didn't need his permission or his blessing. Would it make a difference if he called and said, "I'm happy for you both"?

The phone rang while Geoffrey was considering his options—the customized tone let him know it was Nash. For a brief moment, he considered not answering it at all. But he couldn't hide from Nash forever.

"Hey," he greeted.

"Hey, Geoff. You sound a bit better tonight," Nash said

"I feel a bit better," Geoffrey said.

"That's good. You ever been that drunk before?"

Geoffrey smiled ruefully. "No, not quite that drunk."

"Well, now you know better. Some of us learn that lesson in college."

"I was too busy in college babysitting you," Geoffrey countered. "And being the designated driver."

Nash laughed. "That's true. I guess you have a lot of catching up to do."

"I guess so." Geoffrey paused. "Nash..."

"Geoff..."

Geoff forced a laugh. "You go first."

Now Nash paused. "I...uh...didn't know if you planned to come in to the office tomorrow."

"I thought I might," Geoffrey said carefully.

"You don't have to."

Geoffrey's heart fell. He had gone too far. "Oh."

"I mean," Nash said quickly, "we're going to take the day off tomorrow."

"You're going to take the day off?" Geoffrey knew what those words meant separately, but he didn't quite understand what Nash was telling him.

"Yeah. Sunny thought we could all use a little break, you know? Plus, our schedules are mostly open tomorrow, and when was the last time we had a day off?" Nash asked.

"Today, actually."

"Ok, yes, today," Nash said, and Geoff could hear his smile. "But I mean all three of us."

"We don't normally take days off together."

"Exactly!" Nash exclaimed. "That's it exactly. And don't you think we should?"

Geoffrey had never thought that, actually. But he desperately wanted to make up for his little fit, so at that point, he would agree to anything. "I think that's a good idea."

"Great. We hoped you would say that."

"Did you need my permission to close the office?" Geoffrey asked, confused.

"No, we want...look, can we come by and pick you up tomorrow around ten?"

"Um. Sure."

"Great. Sunny wants to know if you need anything tonight?"

Geoffrey closed his eyes. *I'm happy for them. I'm happy for them. I'm not bothered at all that Sunny is with him right now. That he's calling from his apartment and Sunny is there.* If he told himself that enough, he'd begin to believe it. But even if he couldn't believe it, it was important that Nash didn't think Geoff had a problem.

"Tell her I'm fine. Thank you."

"Good. Look, if you do need anything..."

"I'm fine, Nash. Really. I guess I'll see you tomorrow."

"Not puking, right?"

Geoff forced another laugh. "Right."

Geoffrey hung up the phone, sinking against the couch. He regarded the ceiling thoughtfully, trying to figure out what the hell that entire conversation was about. He would meet them the next morning at ten, and he would do anything they asked him to do, but for the life of him, he couldn't understand what it was all about.

*   *   *

Geoffrey dressed as he would for any day at the office, but lost the tie and jacket after a moment of consideration. Nash had said this would be a day off, so he thought he should try to dress down a bit. As he waited for the minute hand to move forward, he wondered again why he had agreed to this…whatever it was…at all.

Spending an entire day watching them hang all over each other did not sound appealing. Spending an hour didn't sound appealing. He had fluctuated back to being horrified and sick at the thought of Sunny with Nash, and he hoped he could be happy for them once again by the time they arrived.

Geoffrey saw the situation as a challenge. A test. If he could make it through the day without having his heart torn out of his chest, then things could continue as before. He would go to work every day, he would do his best to support Nash and be friendly with Sunny, and he wouldn't give either one of them reason to think that his little bender would become a common occurrence.

Geoffrey always did well on tests. Especially tests he was prepared for. And he spent the whole night trying to prepare himself.

He was sitting by the front window when Nash pulled up in his sleek, black car. They both stepped out, and Geoffrey's heart stopped. Sunny was wearing a short denim skirt that hugged her curves like a second skin. Her legs were long and sleek, nicely shaped and muscled. Her blouse was as tight as the skirt, the buttons at the top hanging open, exposing her ample cleavage. Geoffrey had never seen Sunny dressed so provocatively, and though he knew she had a gorgeous body, this was the first time he had the visual proof.

There wasn't a sight on the planet that could divert his attention from her. Except Nash. Nobody could pull off jeans and a cotton shirt like Nash. Geoffrey knew people who paid hundreds of dollars on clothes to look half as good Nash did in his simple outfit. As Sunny circled the car, he offered his arm, and they approached his door.

Geoffrey whimpered.

He couldn't do this. How was he going to do this? Why would they want to do this to him? They weren't cruel people. And yet, it seemed they had set out specifically to torture him.

Geoffrey's stomach lurched as Nash knocked on the door. *You can do this. It'll be the longest day of your life, but you can do this.*

He glanced at the mirror in the hall to confirm his smile wasn't too strained, too forced. He thought he looked normal. Pleasant, even.

"Hey," Sunny greeted as he opened the door, "ready to go, slugger?"

"Absolutely. Am I dressed appropriately? I didn't know."

"You look great," Nash said.

Geoffrey looked up sharply, unable to believe that the compliment had come from Nash. "I…well…thank you."

"Have you had breakfast yet?" Sunny asked.

"Just some tea," Geoffrey answered, closing and locking the door behind him.

"Perfect. Let's go," Sunny said, looping her arm through his.

"I…" Geoffrey looked down at her smooth, bare arm resting against his. Sunny was casual with contact. She was far more affectionate and touchy-feely than anybody Geoffrey had ever encountered, so this wasn't surprising. Still, she hadn't been sleeping with his best friend the last time she touched him.

Except, maybe she had been sleeping with Nash then. How was he to know? Either way, Nash didn't seem to notice or care, so he allowed them to lead him to the car.

"You can take shotgun," Sunny said, opening the backdoor.

Geoffrey didn't argue. He watched Nash as he settled behind the wheel and started the car, hoping to find some sort of clue. He saw nothing. Nash's face was impassive, and he didn't volunteer any information. Except, occasionally, a tiny smile flitted across his features. It always disappeared quickly, but Geoffrey caught it out of the corner of his eye.

Geoff assumed they were going to a restaurant. But they were driving farther from the center of town where Nash's favorite restaurants were located. He wondered idly if Sunny knew Nash's favorite places to eat. Then he wondered why it even mattered. But when Nash finally parked the car, they were outside the San Antonio Botanical Gardens.

"I thought we were going to eat," Geoff said.

Sunny wrapped her arms around the seat, grabbing his shoulders for a moment. "We are!"

"A picnic," Nash elaborated.

"We're having a *picnic*?" Geoffrey asked. "Seriously? A picnic?"

"Do you have something against picnics?" Sunny asked, and he realized her mouth was far too close to his face.

"No, I don't. I just…can't remember the last time I had a picnic. Actually, I don't think I've ever been on a picnic. Nash, do you go on picnics?" Geoffrey smiled.

"I do now," Nash said, pushing the car door open.

"Good enough for me," Geoffrey muttered, following him.

Nash took a cooler and a basket out of the trunk. Geoff reached over to help, but Sunny batted him away. "I got it."

Before Geoffrey could protest, Nash and Sunny were strolling up the trail. Geoff had no choice but to follow them. Why were they taking him on a picnic? Though, Geoffrey acknowledged, it was a lovely day for a picnic. If he hadn't been concerned about his whole world falling apart, he might have been able to enjoy it. The sun was a soft yellow against a mellow blue sky, birds fluttered overhead, a cool breeze caressed his skin, and as they moved deeper into the gardens, the sweet aroma of flowers made him a little heady.

There were picnic tables in the center of the garden, and as soon as Sunny found one she deemed worthy, she spread a blanket over the rough planks. Nash began systematically unpacking the cooler, revealing a plethora of small delights. Small quiches, fresh bread from the bakery, a variety of cheeses, spread, and chopped fruits, plus a bottle of Geoffrey's favorite juice from Trader Joe's.

"This is really nice," Geoffrey said sincerely.

"It was Sunny's idea."

She smiled at Geoff. "I know what you like."

Geoffrey swallowed hard, her playful smile doing something funny to his insides. "Not as well as you know what Nash likes, I'm sure." As soon as he spoke, Geoffrey's cheeks reddened. "I'm sorry. That was…that was inappropriate."

Sunny shrugged it off. "Sit down. Let me fix you a plate."

"Sunny, I can fix my own plate," Geoff protested.

"But I want to."

"But you don't have to."

"But I *want* to," she insisted, and the look in her eyes told Geoffrey it wouldn't do any good to argue with her.

"Thank you."

Nash merely smiled, settling his bulk on the table's narrow bench. He watched Sunny with patient amusement, the smile never leaving his face. Geoffrey sat across from him with a soft sigh. He recognized that look. He knew it well. Nash was falling for that girl.

"How did the meeting go yesterday?" Geoffrey finally asked.

"Oh," Nash waved his hand, "I don't want to discuss business right now."

"What?"

"I don't want to discuss business right now," Nash repeated.

"Yes, I heard you the first time. I just don't believe you," Geoffrey said.

"Well, I'm not kidding today."

Geoffrey's eyes widened with alarm. "Oh, my God, it was that bad? I'm sorry, Nash. I should have gone over those numbers with you. In fact, I should have gone over the entire proposal before I left. I shouldn't have left. The whole world shouldn't come crashing to a halt just because I can't…"

Nash held up his hands, cutting off Geoffrey's speech. "It was fine. It went great. They really liked your proposal, and the numbers all checked out. I promise. I just…want to relax a bit. We've all been a bit high-strung lately."

Geoffrey's relaxed slightly. "Yeah. A bit high-strung."

Sunny smirked and set his plate in front of him. "You like finger food, right?"

"Yeah, I guess…"

Sunny popped a piece of cheese in his mouth while he was speaking, smiling at his grunt of surprise. "So do I."

Geoffrey turned helpless eyes toward Nash, but he was too busy pouring a cup of juice to pay attention to what Sunny was doing.

"I'm glad things went well," Geoffrey said, after swallowing his cheese. "I am sorry, Nash. That was irresponsible of me, and it won't happen again."

"I know," Nash said, passing him a cup. "Now are you going to enjoy the picnic that Sunny prepared or what?"

Geoffrey smiled, smoothing a thin layer of strawberry spread over his bread. Nash smiled indulgently at Sunny as she passed him his plate, and Geoffrey could barely taste his food. It was a shame that his tongue refused to cooperate, because he thought the food did look very delicious. Nash certainly seemed to be enjoying it. And Sunny seemed to enjoy watching Nash enjoy it.

Geoff needed a moment to regroup. In a stroke of brilliance, he remembered the outhouses near the gate. "I need to excuse myself for a moment."

Nash popped a small butter cookie in his mouth and nodded. "We'll be here."

Geoffrey dragged his feet along the trail they had followed to the table, stalled in the bathroom as long as he could, and shuffled back. He took a different path, one that would bring him around to the table from the back. As he stepped through the plants, he caught sight of Nash and Sunny, and it was like seeing them again for the first time. Sunny was smashed against his chest, and Nash's hands were flat against her back. Geoffrey paused, hanging back, and tried to ignore the lump forming in his throat. He couldn't move. He was rooted to the spot, torn between the urge to run and the urge to stay right there and watch.

It hurt to watch, but it felt a little good, too. They were gorgeous together, dark-haired deities clinging to each other. Something stirred in his groin, but died as soon as he felt it. There was too much confusion, too much unrecognized longing, and still, he couldn't move. If he approached them, they would stop. But he had nowhere to run.

After several seconds of hesitation, Geoffrey finally forced himself to move. He stepped into the clearing, coughing lightly as he approached, and they jumped apart like guilty children. He smiled tightly as he sat on the bench again, but he didn't look at either one of them. Instead, he concentrated on the food he really didn't want to eat, and wondered about what happened to being happy for them.

"Sorry, Geoffrey. We, uh, didn't see you," Nash said softly.

"Yeah." That was the problem, wasn't it? They never saw him.

Sunny moved to his side, sliding onto the bench and sitting a little too close. She touched his arm with light fingers, and Geoffrey flinched, pulling away like she had burned him. Sunny's eyes widened in shock, and Geoffrey thought he saw genuine hurt in their brown depths.

"Sorry," he muttered. "You startled me."

Tension settled over the table, coating all the food until it was waxy and unappealing. Geoffrey kept eating, because he didn't know what else to do. He could feel both Nash and Sunny watching him, and he wanted to scream at them to stop, but he didn't make the effort. Out of the corner of his eye, he saw Nash reach across the table to rest his hand on top of Sunny's—a casual, comforting gesture. Like Geoffrey was the jerk, and Sunny needed to be coddled.

Maybe he was the jerk.

"I appreciate the food," Geoff said, pushing himself to his feet. "I do. And thank you for thinking of me, but I'd like to go home now."

"Geoffrey..." Sunny started.

"I hope you'll forgive me if I wait at the car," he said, using his most apologetic smile.

"Go ahead," Nash said.

Geoffrey nodded, foolishly thinking that they were going to let him escape again, but he should have known better. He had known Nash for a decade, and he knew how to read the other man. Still, it came as a surprise when Nash caught up with him thirty feet later and grabbed his arm.

"We need to talk," he said, pulling Geoffrey off the trail into a thicket of something purple and sweet.

"I guess so."

Nash took off his shades and folded his arms. They stood with only a few feet separating them, but Geoffrey had never felt so distant from his friend. Nothing like this had ever happened to them before, and Geoff didn't know where to start.

"I'm sorry," he said, his eyes averted from Nash. "I'm not handling this very well."

"I should be the one apologizing," Nash replied.

"You? You haven't done anything wrong."

"Yes, I have. I really have, Geoffrey, and I'm sorry. I knew that you liked her, but when it happened, I just wasn't thinking."

Geoffrey swallowed. "How did...when?"

"About a month ago. She stayed late with me to work on the goddamned filing. I don't know how it happened, Geoff. One minute, we were trying to figure out which Smith file was which, and the next we were kissing, and then..."

"A month?" Geoffrey felt weak. "You've been...for a month? Nash, why didn't you tell me? Didn't you think I would have wanted to know? Didn't you think I deserved to know?"

"I didn't want to hurt you," he admitted.

"And finding out this way was less painful?" Geoffrey asked.

"I'm sorry," Nash said helplessly.

Geoffrey sighed. "I keep telling myself that I'm happy for the two of you. If you're happy, I am. I keep telling myself that it doesn't matter, and I'll get used to it, but..."

"It doesn't work out that way?"

"It doesn't seem to." Geoffrey moved to a tree, leaning his shoulder against the trunk with his back to Nash. "I don't know what today was about, but I'm sorry I ruined your picnic."

"It was about you."

Geoffrey looked over his shoulder, and Nash was much closer than he thought. "What?"

"We were scared," Nash admitted. "After yesterday. We thought we were going to lose you. Neither one of us wants that."

Geoffrey shook his head. "That was childish of me, Nash, and I truly am sorry. I didn't mean to tell you that I quit. It was just…the heat of the moment. I don't intend to sell my part of the firm. Well, unless you want me to at this point."

"No."

Geoff turned to rest his back against the trunk, surprised by Nash's vehemence. "Still not certain about those Bowie numbers?"

"That's not…I mean, I don't want you to leave the firm either, but that's not what we were really worried about. We don't want to lose you, Geoffrey, from our lives."

Now Nash was standing toe to toe with him, and the sheer strength of his will forced Geoffrey to look at him. "I can't see you two like that, Nash. What we've done together, what we've built, is too important for me to walk away from it all. But I can't watch you two. I know I should just deal with it, but I can't."

"Why?" Nash asked softly, as though he actually expected Geoffrey to answer him.

"Why? Nash…" Geoffrey paused, unsure of what to say. He had already made a massive ass of himself that morning; he might as well go the distance. "Because it's looking at everything I've ever wanted and nothing I can ever have."

"Everything?" Nash said, as though he wasn't familiar with the word.

"Everything."

"Geoffrey…"

And then the world was frozen around him. Time stopped. His heart stopped. Nash's mouth was on his, his hands gripping Geoffrey's shoulders. This was something Geoffrey had thought about, a fantasy he had forced himself to forget, and now he didn't know how to react. His body betrayed him, his mind left him, and he was left as stiff and dumb as a mannequin while Nash continued to tease his mouth.

Finally, his lungs remembered how to work and forced him to gasp. That slight movement was enough to re-awaken his body, and he moved forward, into Nash's embrace and opened his lips to deepen the kiss. They stumbled back, Geoffrey pushing until Nash hit the tree behind him. The kiss moved from something hesitant, to something demanding, both of them giving in to an urge that had been dogging them for over ten years.

The kiss slowed, losing that desperate edge, and Nash put his hands on Geoffrey's hips, pulling him closer. Geoffrey could taste the sweet fruit juice on Nash's lips, and something else, something a bit bitter. He knew it was Sunny. He knew she could be coming to look for them at any minute, and knew what he was doing was wrong. So wrong. But desire flooded his body and he couldn't make himself stop. He was dying for it, dying for the attention, dying to explore every bit of Nash's mouth, and then further, to know every inch of his body.

"You've been wanting to do that for awhile," Nash murmured when Geoffrey finally lifted his head, but he didn't step away.

"Yeah, awhile," Geoffrey agreed.

"Why didn't you?"

Geoffrey's eyes widened. "Why didn't I slam you against a wall and kiss you? Did I have any reason to think you'd welcome that sort of treatment?"

"You really are oblivious, aren't you?" Nash asked, but not unkindly.

"Who said I was oblivious?"

"Me," Sunny said from behind him.

Geoffrey stiffened, taking a halting step backward. He didn't want to turn to face her. How could he explain pushing her boyfriend against the tree and devouring his mouth? He looked at Nash helplessly, but Nash didn't seem concerned at all.

In fact, he was smiling.

"I owe you five dollars, I guess," Nash said, pushing away from the tree.

Geoffrey looked over his shoulder to see Sunny holding out her hand and smirking. "Five dollars? Oblivious? What?"

"I told Nash you had a thing for him," Sunny explained, still looking far too pleased with herself. "Guess I was right."

"I guess you were," Geoff muttered. What was this? It wasn't enough to tear his heart out, they had to take bets on what hurt the most? He wiped his mouth with the back of his hand. "Don't spend it all in one place."

"Geoffrey," Nash took his arm, as if he could sense Geoff's impulse to flee. "Come back to my place with us."

"What?"

Sunny took a step forward with an almost predatory smile. "We want you, Geoffrey."

Now this was just too much. His brain refused to accept that the scene playing out before him was reality. Perhaps he was still drunk, passed out in the bathroom, and locked in an endless dream. No, he corrected himself, this wouldn't be a dream. This was a nightmare.

"I don't…I don't understand…" Geoffrey finally said, his eyes darting to Nash for clues. Nash, his old friend. Nash, the man he could read like a book. Nash, the person he had followed around in college like a lost puppy desperately waiting for a single crumb of affection. But Nash looked back with an unfamiliar light in his eyes.

That's what it looks like to be wanted. To be wanted by him.

"I think you do," Sunny murmured, pushing her body against his.

And the world came to a grinding halt for the second time in ten minutes. She tasted delicious. And she felt delicious. Her mouth was like warmed fruit, her hands small and firm against his face as she stretched to deepen the kiss. His arms went around her on their own accord, locking her against him. He could feel Nash's gaze on them, hear the other man's sudden intake of breath, and like before, he knew he was wrong.

Like before, he didn't care.

Why are they doing this to me?

It didn't make sense, the way she tasted of Nash, the way he knew it. And, God, he could understand now. Understand Nash's confusion, understand how they could go from searching for a file to kissing to something much more. Because nobody kissed like Sunny. He didn't know if she had practice, or if it was an innate skill. Some fortunate talent she was born with. Her mouth was sinful against his, a dark red promise of delights and pleasures that he could barely conceive of.

Sunny shocked him by slipping her hand between their bodies and over his growing erection. She pulled away from the kiss, her eyes mirroring his surprise.

"Maybe I owe Nash five bucks," she said, arching her eyebrow.

"Maybe it's a wash," Geoffrey replied.

Sunny shook her head. "I don't understand, Geoff. I mean, if you liked me, why didn't you…you know?"

"What?"

"Do something about it? Ask me out? Anything?"

"Why didn't I what? Sunny…I didn't think…I mean, I didn't know if my advances were welcome."

She gaped at him, and then slapped him on the chest. "I did everything except blow you under your desk. What did I have to do?

Send a singing telegram?"

Geoffrey blinked. "This is…Sunny, I had no idea. I just thought you were…friendly. Why would you be interested in me?"

Sunny looked to Nash, exasperated. "Has he always been like this?"

"He never got laid in college, despite some of my best efforts." Nash shrugged. "Make of that what you will."

Geoffrey stepped back, putting as much distance between them and himself as he could in the small clearing. The sun was almost at its zenith now, leaving no shadows or relief from its bright glare. The heat poured over them, but Geoffrey didn't know if the flush of his skin was from that or bewildered embarrassment.

"What right do you have to criticize me about being oblivious?" Geoffrey demanded, looking at Nash. "How can you say I'm oblivious when I've loved you as long as I've known you and you never even noticed?"

Now it was Nash's turn to look shocked, and before the horror struck him, Geoffrey was deeply satisfied.

"Can we finish this conversation somewhere else?" Nash asked, looking over his shoulder to an approaching family. "I don't think this is an appropriate place."

Geoffrey didn't think he could tolerate being with the two of them any longer. The trip home, trapped in Nash's car and at his mercy, would be excruciating. He didn't know if he could blame it on the sun, or the remnants of the alcohol, or the shock of both kisses, but he had just blurted a secret that he'd vowed would go to the grave with him. A secret that could change everything, and probably not for the better. A secret that, up until two days ago, Geoffrey thought was insignificant because he was *over* Nash and his childish crush, damn it.

"I think you're right," Sunny said, before turning pleading eyes to Geoff. "I know this is really…weird, Geoff, but I do think we should talk about this. Please?"

"I…" He sighed, unable to deny her anything when she looked at him like that. "Yeah. Okay."

"Great. Let's go gather up the food and get out of here."

Geoffrey nodded, following them back to the table. This was going to be a very long day. Geoffrey didn't know if he was prepared for that.

CHAPTER 4

Geoffrey was saved from finishing the conversation by the insistent ring of his phone, of Nash's phone, and of Sunny's pager. Even as Nash checked his messages, Geoffrey knew exactly who it was and what she wanted. Claire Bowie was a sharp lady and a great client, but she was very demanding of their time.

"Back to the office?" Geoffrey asked, once Nash tucked his phone away.

Nash looked torn. Geoffrey could see the battle in his eyes, and he wanted to shake him. Whatever drama they were acting out did not trump their clients' welfare.

"It's not really an emergency," Nash hedged.

"It's never really an emergency with her," Geoffrey pointed out. "That doesn't mean she should be ignored."

"He's right," Sunny said, an unlikely ally. "Besides, she *won't* be ignored. She'll just keep paging and keep calling until she makes us crazy."

Nash looked at Sunny through the rearview mirror and nodded. "Yeah. You're right." He looked at Geoff. "She's actually been trying to get a hold of you."

"That's fine. Drop me off at home so I can change."

He could tell that Nash wanted to argue, but Nash kept it to himself and put the car into gear. The ride to Geoffrey's house passed in silence, and that was fine with him. He pushed the scene between the three of them out of his mind and concentrated on the meeting with

Claire, trying to figure out what she could need. No doubt, just quiet assurances that the project wouldn't fall through, that it would happen by the deadline, and everything would be fine. It wasn't an uncommon need, and Geoffrey often handled this side of the meetings.

"We'll meet you at the office," Nash said as he pulled to a stop.

"If you think it's necessary," Geoffrey said, before exiting the car. He knew he should have said something more, but he slammed the door before they could stop him.

He called Claire to set up a meeting for an hour later before changing. He knew that he was only putting off the inevitable, but a part of him hoped that somehow everything could be reset to normal by the time he reached the office. Perhaps Nash and Sunny would realize that whatever they wanted from him was unreasonable. Or maybe they'd realize they didn't want anything from him at all. Maybe over drinks they could agree to forget about the whole morning, like civilized people.

Except, he wasn't entirely sure he wanted to forget the whole morning. Despite his bewilderment, the few minutes when he was touching them, kissing them, had been like a dream come true. And if they wanted him, wanted more of that, did he really have the wherewithal to turn it down?

An hour after Nash dropped him off, Geoffrey was waiting for Claire at the office, his mind still in turmoil. But as soon as she walked into the door, he shifted gears easily, shedding his confusion to be the diplomatic, reassuring consultant their clients needed.

"Geoffrey," Claire greeted, extending her hand as he stood. "I tried to call the office earlier. Imagine my surprise when nobody answered the phone."

"Yes, unfortunately, I was out of the office this morning," he said, shaking her hand before leading her to the conference room.

She looked around. "Where's Sunny and Nash?" Her eyes widened. "Were you closed today? Oh, I'm sorry. I wouldn't have disturbed you if I knew it was a day off. It's not some sort of holiday, is it? I didn't see anything marked on the calendar."

"No holiday," he assured her. "And it was no trouble. Besides, you know we're always here when you need us."

"I don't expect you to be at my beck and call," Claire said as Geoffrey shut the door behind them. She settled near the head of the oval desk and pulled several files out of her bag. "I just had a few questions. I suppose they could have waited."

"Nonsense," Geoffrey said, sitting beside her with his own files. "Now let's see what you've got."

* * *

Nash watched Geoffrey and Claire work through the window, his arms crossed. Geoffrey was smiling, friendly and, occasionally, he laughed at something Claire said. Claire, for her part, was equally at ease with him.

"How's it going in there?" Sunny asked.

"He's got her eating out of his hand," Nash said, accepting the cup of coffee she offered. "She's never that easygoing with me."

"Jealous?"

"No. Well, yes, a little. I'm not sure how he does that."

"There's just something about him that people respond to," Sunny observed. She took Nash's hand and led him to his office. "Not that there isn't something about you that people respond to."

"Thanks." He sat heavily in his chair while she perched on the corner of his desk. "Why do I have an office?"

Sunny blinked. "Because you're the boss?"

"Geoff deserves an office," Nash pointed out.

"I thought Geoffrey didn't want an office. He likes to be there to greet the clients," Sunny reminded him.

Nash fidgeted with the pens on his desk, unable to meet Sunny's eyes. "He's a good kisser, isn't he?"

"He is."

"It's funny the things you can find out about people," he murmured.

"Like the fact that he loves you?" Sunny asked, never one to leave things unsaid.

Nash sighed. Exactly like that. How could he have not known? He had spent more time with Geoffrey than he spent with his own family. Sometimes he forgot that Geoffrey wasn't his family. They had been through so much together, and it had never occurred to him that Geoffrey waded through that shit for him. Because he loved him.

"Do you love him?" Sunny asked softly.

"I don't know."

Which was the closest thing to the truth that Nash could find. He knew that he didn't want to think about a life without Geoff. He knew that he'd be lost if Geoffrey followed through with his threat and left him, left the business. But he also knew that he had never been happier than in the past month with Sunny.

He didn't understand how things could get so complicated. Just three days ago, everything was fine. Now, it was all tied up in knots, and short of slicing through it all with a sword, Nash didn't know how to untangle everything. He felt like no matter what he said, no matter what he thought, he'd hurt somebody. He couldn't stand to hurt Geoffrey, and he'd rather cut his own hand off than hurt Sunny.

"I didn't mean to get you caught in the middle of this," Nash said, looking at her through his lashes.

"It was my idea," Sunny reminded him. "All of this was my idea. I kissed you first, and I suggested we try to…seduce Geoffrey."

"Yeah, but I kissed Geoffrey first. And I ignored his feelings for years…"

"Can you ignore something you didn't know existed?" Sunny asked.

"Apparently."

"I think you're being too hard on yourself," Sunny said, moving to stand in front of him. If Claire weren't just across the hall, he'd pull her into his lap.

"I don't think so." He took her hand, rubbing his thumb over her knuckles. "What do you want to do?"

"What do you mean?" Sunny asked.

"Do you want to tell us both to fuck off? Do you want to make Geoffrey come in here and work this out? Do you want me to let him leave? Should we just pretend none of this ever happened and go back to the way things were before?" Nash asked, scared to find out the answers to any of those questions.

"You two are the greatest guys I know. I don't want to do anything to hurt either one of you. I don't want to come between you, either. I'll leave before Geoffrey does," Sunny announced.

"No…"

She touched his lips with the tip of her finger. "Yes. But maybe it won't come to that. I think we can work this out if we take a bit of time."

"I still wish I hadn't put you in the middle of this."

"You can make it up to me later," Sunny promised.

CHAPTER 5

Geoffrey could still remember the first time he fantasized about Nash. He still remembered what led to the fantasy, what the fantasy entailed, how hard he came, and how mortified he felt afterward. But when it came to Nash, there wasn't a second of their friendship he didn't remember. He horded every moment, every act, every smile, as though maybe he'd lose it all without warning.

Nash had walked into his life, and into him, on a cool autumn morning. It had been very early, and the campus had been empty. If he had been walking a foot to the right, or Nash had taken a different route to the business building, they never would have met. But Nash had been in a hurry, his head down, and he had plowed right into Geoffrey. Geoff's glasses almost went flying, his books slipped, and when he looked up, he was in lust.

The love would come later.

But it was that first fantasy that Geoffrey kept coming back to as he tried to focus on Claire's concerns. That first fantasy of the two of them. It had been so secret, so frantic. It was much later that Geoffrey had learned to take his time with the fantasies, because they were all he had. And later still when he forced himself to stop, because instead of making things easier, they were making things so much worse.

Geoffrey had been alone in his dorm room. His roommate, Rich, had been out with his girlfriend. That's what had started it all. Geoffrey thought of Rich and his little girlfriend, Kat, and the two of them in the backseat of his Chevy. Then he wondered if Nash had a girlfriend. And then he hoped that maybe Nash didn't have a *girlfriend*. Maybe Nash was attracted to men. Why not? After all, it was his fantasy. And maybe Nash was attracted to *him*.

The thought had sent a shiver down his spine, directly to his cock.

Geoffrey had known that it would be easy enough to get Nash alone. Maybe they would share a few beers. Geoffrey didn't have any seduction techniques then—who was he kidding? He didn't have any seduction techniques now, over ten years later. But in his fantasy, he disposed of the seduction, of the dance, and got right to the part where Nash was on top of him, pinning him to his chair.

Right to the part where he opened his mouth to Nash's kiss without hesitation, drinking in the taste of him, losing himself in the other man's touch, and the pressure of his lips, and the way he smelled—a slightly spicy cologne mingled with his sweat and maybe the faint hint of cigarettes.

"The problem is that I don't think we can do this by the end of the year."

Geoffrey's head snapped up. Claire was looking at him expectantly. He had an answer for this. He had an answer for all her concerns. But it took him a few minutes to find it, buried somewhere behind the heated thoughts of Nash.

"Of course, we can have it finished by the end of the year," Geoffrey assured her. "This is a high priority for us."

"Oh, I never meant to imply it wasn't," she said quickly.

His hands sneak up, and he grips Nash's shoulders, holding him close and bracing himself. Nash's tongue sweeps through his mouth with hunger, as though he had never tasted anything so sweet, or kissed anybody with so much desire. Geoffrey responds without hesitation. He doesn't hold anything back from Nash, or from the kiss. He wants Nash to know that he's serious, that he wants him, that he's prepared to sacrifice his body to Nash's pleasure.

Geoffrey smiled. "We can arrange to have weekly meetings, if you'd like. It might be a little difficult to find a time that works for both of us, but I would be more than happy to accommodate you."

Claire brightened. "I think that would help with the anxiety. You know, ever since I took over this project, I feel like I've been out of my league. I *told* Scott that I'd rather just manage the store and deal with the inventory."

"Well, personally, I think Mr. Scott was right to give you the task. You've been wonderful to work with. Some people can be...clueless."

They kiss for what could be hours. Sometimes the kisses are hard, their teeth clashing, their tongues dueling. These kisses leave Geoffrey's lips bruised, and his head spinning. Sometimes, the kisses are gentle, slow. The kisses are soft caresses, their mouths sealed together, their tongues searching and languid. These kisses make Geoffrey ache. The make the bottoms of his feet tingle. Nash is a good kisser, an expert at drawing forth soft sighs, desperate moans, and honing general desire to a very fine, very specific thing.

Claire laughed. "I feel more than a little clueless. That's why I'm pestering you all the time."

Geoffrey shook his head. He knew that the clueless little girl routine was just that—a routine. But to what end? She had played this card once or twice, but never as blatantly. He didn't know what she could want from him that he wasn't already giving her.

"Please, you're hardly pestering us. You've hired our firm to do a job, and we're not happy unless you are."

Geoffrey wants to feel Nash's mouth everywhere. He wants to feel the heat of his breath on his throat, on his chest, on his stomach and his thighs, and then finally, wrapped around his cock. He wants to melt beneath Nash's tongue, wants to bury his hands through the other man's short, dark hair, wants Nash to look at him with dark eyes as he takes Geoffrey's cock into his mouth, past his lips, and down his throat.

Claire leaned forward, and the top of her shirt pulled tight over her breasts. Her red hair hung in loose curls around her face, and Geoffrey tried to focus on her, but he was losing track of himself. A part of his mind was completely gone, turned over to the fantasy that insisted on unraveling itself in his head. Usually, he could pull those thoughts back, put them under control. But Nash had kissed him, only two hours ago, and for the first time, his fantasies had a little substance.

"I was wondering," Claire started. "If maybe, a few of our meetings couldn't be over dinner?"

He knows Nash can feel his erection pressed against his thigh. He can feel Nash's. It seems to grow harder with each kiss and caress, and it's not long before Geoffrey feels compelled to reach for him. He unzips Nash's jeans—his fingers are always quick and sure—and he wraps his hand around Nash's shaft. They both sigh with the relief of the contact.

Nash is hard and long. Geoffrey strokes him slowly, becoming accustomed to the heat and texture of his skin. His fingers trace the outline of his shaft, memorizing the feel of it, memorizing the sensitive points that make it jump in his hand, memorizing each moan and gasp that comes from Nash's throat.

Geoffrey tilted his head, confused. "Well, I suppose that wouldn't be a problem if a later meeting works better for you. I'll have to check with Sunny."

"Oh? Why?"

Geoffrey frowned. "Because she makes my schedule. I'd have to clear any possible meetings with Sunny."

Claire laughed, and she sounded a bit nervous to Geoffrey. "Oh, I thought you meant something else."

Geoffrey gently pushes Nash's weight off of him. Nash is still above him, but now his feet touch the floor, and his hands brace on the arms of Geoffrey's chair. Geoffrey slides down the plush cushions until he's sitting on the floor, and Nash's perfect cock is in front of his face, just an inch from his watering mouth.

Geoffrey knows what he wants. He knows he wants Nash to touch him and kiss him, knows he wants Nash to fuck him. But before any of that could happen, Geoffrey needs to taste him. He needs to know how Nash feels against his tongue and sliding down his throat. He needs to know how Nash sounds when pleasure is overtaking him. Does he moan when he comes? Does he shout? Is he silent?

He was getting a little tired of this conversation. It was difficult enough to follow Claire's sometimes erratic way of thinking when he was paying full attention. And he most certainly was not giving her his full attention. Or even half of his attention. He marveled that he could have a conversation with her at all, when his cock was semi-erect and his thoughts were rushing forward like a steam engine out of control.

"What else?" he asked, for something to say.

Geoffrey's tongue darts out to sample the clear pre-come that glistens on the tip of Nash's head, and they both whimper slightly. Nash spreads his legs further, bracing himself for more, and Geoffrey's hand goes to his heavy balls. He rolls them between his fingers gently, sensitive to any signals from Nash. Every signal he senses gives him one simple demand—continue.

So Geoffrey does. He slides his lips over Nash's cock, his tongue slipping along his head and his shaft. He pushes forward, and pulls Nash toward him, and it's not long until his nose is buried in the coarse hairs at the base of Nash's cock, and his throat is relaxed to accommodate Nash's length, and his own erection is painful against his tight jeans, and he's lost in heat, the experience, the need, the hunger, the sound of his own name tumbling from Nash's lips in frantic pleas.

"Oh...I mean, I thought you had to get her approval to go out," Claire said and laughed lightly.

"Out? Like on a date?" he asked slowly.

"Well, yeah."

Geoffrey wants Nash to come undone for him. He wants Nash to forget every lover he's ever had. He wants Nash to be lost, out of his mind. He wants Nash to fuck his face, to rock his hips forward, to push his cock down his throat. He grips Nash's hips, pulls him back until his head is against the tip of Geoffrey's tongue, and then pushes him forward again. He does that twice more before Nash understands, and then Geoffrey doesn't have to do anything except hold him, swallow him, be used by him.

"I don't date my clients, Ms. Bowie," Geoffrey said in a clipped tone.

She reared back, and he was afraid he offended her. He rushed to explain.

"I would. Date you. If you were interested, that is. And you weren't a client. I didn't misunderstand you, did I?"

She smiled again, and he could tell that if there was offense, she had forgiven him. "You didn't misunderstand. I was actually trying to lead up to a favor."

"A favor?"

Geoffrey's cock is throbbing, his groin is tight, his lower stomach feels heavy. He's in utter torment, as more pre-come spills from Nash's cock and coats his tongue. And the torment makes it better. That desire, so simple, so pointed, makes Nash taste better. That lust makes his moans sweeter. And when Nash begins to gasp his name, saying it over and over again, "Geoffrey, Geoff...Geoff...oh God, Geoffrey..." he thinks he'll come in his pants.

"Yes, I know this is very, very short notice. And you're probably busy. And I don't really have any right to expect you to do it. You know what? Never mind. Forget I brought it up."

Now the helpless little girl routine wasn't such an act. He could tell she was genuinely nervous about something. "No, please. If I can help in anyway, I will."

Geoffrey does come when Nash does. He can feel it building in Nash, and his fingers tighten on his hips. He's prepared to swallow every drop, to suck on him until there's nothing left, and then lick him until he's completely clean. He doesn't want to lose a single second with Nash. He wants to take advantage of every moment, every chance to taste him, every chance to show Nash how much he wants him.

Geoffrey wished he could reach under the table and unzip his pants. He shifted his weight, hoping that would ease the pressure, but it didn't make any noticeable difference.

When Nash thrusts forward for the final time, Geoffrey is ready for him. The hot jizz explodes in his mouth, and he quickly swallows, careful not to choke. The taste of Nash's come on his tongue, the feel of it at the back of his throat, triggers Geoffrey's orgasm. His hips jerk forward, even as Nash begins to pull away, dragging his semi-erect cock through Geoffrey's lips one last time.

That fantasy was still highly effective. There were variations on the theme, but when Geoffrey wanted to come fast—and when he wasn't living in deep denial—that one always did the trick. But it also left him oddly unsatisfied and deeply curious. He knew what Nash looked like naked, so that part of the fantasy was always accurate. But the rest of the details were pure conjecture. And Geoffrey was prepared for the fact that they always would be pure conjecture.

But now he had the chance to know.

It would be so easy to go home with Nash and Sunny after his meeting. It would be so easy to spend the afternoon, the night, and all the next day indulging each and every fantasy. He even had a few fantasies that involved both of them, though he thought about those on only rare occasions. It would be so easy, so what was stopping him?

Geoffrey couldn't pinpoint the source of his anxiety. There were too many factors, too many considerations, too many ways things could go wrong. Too many lonely nights to convince himself that he was alone, that he'd always be alone, that he needed to accept that. And he had accepted that, because he could never have what he really wanted.

But now Nash was telling him he could. And Sunny's kiss was still resting on his lips, like a butterfly with fragile wings.

"…and of course, it would be better if I didn't show up alone."

Geoffrey blinked. Then blinked again. Claire was looking at him like she expected him to agree to…something.

Oh fuck.

"I'm sorry, I didn't catch that last part," he said, trying on his most charming smile. Or what he thought might have been a charming smile.

"Scott is having a small party tonight to celebrate the opening of the new store. I know, the opening isn't for some time yet, but he's really just celebrating the fact that he's finally got the lease secure. I thought maybe since you're the one who made that happen, you'd like to accompany me?"

"Well, Nash's really done more…"

"I'd like it to be you," Claire said softly.

Geoffrey hesitated. They were waiting for him outside. Waiting for him to go home with them. And he thought maybe he wanted to, except…

He had told Nash that he loved him.

Had loved him for years.

"I don't have anything on my schedule tonight," Geoffrey said. "I'd love to escort you."

Claire beamed, and she looked radiant. "Fantastic. It's at eight, at the new location. There's a bar around the corner. Maybe we could meet there a little early for drinks?"

"Sounds lovely," Geoffrey agreed.

CHAPTER 6

"I just don't understand why you need to meet with her tonight, too," Nash said, sitting on the edge of Geoffrey's bed. Nash had been in his room before, several times. Had even slept there once or twice, but now it was different. Now he was dominating the space, and making Geoffrey uncomfortable. More so.

"Because she asked me to," Geoffrey said, for probably the tenth time. "I don't understand why you needed to follow me home."

"Because I wanted to talk to you. I thought we were going to…talk."

Geoffrey selected a blue tie from his closet and draped it over his neck. "We will talk, Nash. But right now isn't a good time."

In honesty, he didn't think any time would be a *good* time. If he could continue to avoid the situation, he'd be happy. But he'd seen this look in Nash's eyes before. It was usually reserved for impossible clients and difficult problems. It was the look that always meant he was about to throw all his considerable resources behind the effort.

Geoffrey didn't know what to make of that. Confusion was becoming his default mental state.

"It seems like we've missed a lot of good times."

Geoffrey looked up sharply. "What?"

"Maybe I should go now," Nash said, standing up.

Geoffrey waited just a beat before the familiar edge of disappointment cut him. He wanted nothing more than for Nash to leave him alone, except now that Nash was leaving. Now he only wanted to ask the other man to stay.

"Nash…"

"That's why you never dated anybody in college, isn't it?" Nash asked.

"I…what?"

"What you said…" Nash rubbed the back of his neck. "That's why you never dated anybody in college."

"What…oh." Geoffrey turned back to the mirror and began to knot his tie. "Yeah."

"Jesus, Geoff…"

Geoffrey sighed softly. He thought maybe he could keep Nash at bay, but clearly, they were *talking about this now*. Even though Geoffrey didn't really have too much that he wanted to say.

"I just really didn't know," Nash said.

"Yes, well, I didn't want you to know," Geoffrey said, trying to sound matter-of-fact.

"Why not?"

Because I wanted to avoid scenes like this. Geoffrey straightened the knot and smoothed his hair back. He selected a thin pair of wire-frame glasses. He only wore them when he went out on important functions.

"Geoffrey, why didn't you say something?"

Geoffrey thought Nash missed his calling as a lawyer. The qualities Geoffrey found so attractive in Nash were very annoying when they were used against him.

"Because our friendship, and later, our business, was more important to me," Geoffrey answered honestly, without turning around or looking at him. He walked to the closet, picking out a pair of black shoes.

"Geoffrey…" Nash gripped his shoulder and forced him to turn around. "No matter what, we're always going to be friends. You're a part of my life. Maybe the most important part of my life."

Geoffrey knew him well enough to know when he was lying, and that wasn't a lie. He swallowed hard and nodded. He didn't know what he could say though, didn't know how he was supposed to respond. The one thing that seemed to be a constant in his life was the belief that Nash didn't need him nearly as much as he needed Nash. And now even that was thrown into doubt.

"I have to go now," Geoff murmured.

"Please come by tonight," Nash said, his hand still on Geoffrey's shoulder.

"Wouldn't it just be easier to let everything drop?" Geoffrey asked.

"Yeah, it would. It'd be easier if we woke up tomorrow morning pretending that none of this happened. And you can come to work every day, secretly miserable. And I can pretend that I don't notice, that it doesn't bother me. And Sunny can continue to sneak into my office when you go to lunch—if she doesn't just decide to leave completely. That sounds like a fair solution to everybody."

Geoffrey almost smiled. "So maybe my policy of avoidance and denial isn't going to work this time?"

"As far as policies go, it's not a bad one," Nash conceded. "But I think things have gotten too complicated to continue that way."

Geoffrey nodded, noticing for the first time how hot Nash's hand was on his shoulder. Only inches separated them, and it seemed like every inch of his body was attracted to Nash's. If he relaxed his guard or surrendered any of his control, he would close the space between them. He would press his chest against Nash's and revel in the heat and the strength and he didn't even imagine doing anything else. No kissing, no groping, no hungry fingers. Just an embrace.

"Do you want to continue your policy of avoidance and denial?" Nash asked softly.

"It was working pretty well. I was happy."

"Were you? Really?"

"Yeah, I really was. Why shouldn't I be? Because I didn't have everything I once wanted? I'm not greedy." He felt greedy. He felt more greedy in that moment than at any other point in his life. He wanted to push Nash to his bed. He wanted to strip him of his clothes, wanted to finally touch him.

Geoffrey thought it was interesting that he wanted Nash as much now as he ever had. Weren't these urges supposed to fade after a decade?

"Everything you once wanted? What do you want now?"

They were on dangerous ground. A veritable minefield. He might be okay if he understood what Nash wanted from him, but even after this morning, he wasn't sure. But why not try a little honesty? Just to see what happened?

He gripped the front of Nash's shirt and gently pulled him forward. Nash didn't resist at all. Geoffrey had a sudden flash to his fantasy, where they skipped the awkwardness, the seduction, and got right to the part where they were kissing. Maybe he could make it happen here?

After all, Nash had kissed him that morning without warning, and he thought they both found the actual physical experience very pleasurable, even if it sent his mind and emotions into tumult.

Nash's lips were dry and warm. Geoffrey only brushed his mouth. It was hardly a kiss at all. It was just a small taste, a little sip of possibilities. Nash might have deepened the kiss. Or he might have pulled away. Geoffrey didn't have the chance to find out before Nash's cell phone rang.

Geoffrey stepped back quickly, like Nash had kicked him. Nash looked at him a little helplessly before he pulled the phone from his pocket.

"I have to answer this."

"I know."

"I'm really starting to hate this job, by the way," Nash murmured before bringing the phone to his ear.

Geoffrey thought the obvious answer was not to give his private cell number out to clients. But he did the same thing, so he didn't really have room to talk. After a moment of listening, he was able to figure out who had called, and even what the emergency was. Nash's face was clouded with anger…and maybe regret?

Geoffrey shook his head. He was reading into it. He resumed getting dressed as though he had never been interrupted at all. He would be a little late for meeting Claire, but he supposed she might forgive him. And maybe he had the right to be less than punctual when his entire world was spinning off its axis.

He was ready to walk out the door when Nash finally hung up the phone.

"Come over tonight."

"I'll call." It was as much as Geoffrey was willing to promise.

Nash hesitated a moment before nodding. "Fine."

"Come on, I'll walk you to your car."

Geoffrey was careful to keep an arm's length distance between them as they walked out the door. Clearly, he couldn't trust himself around Nash. And he knew as long as Nash encouraged him, it would only get worse.

*   *   *

Claire was a beautiful woman. And when she dressed up, she was stunning. She wore a slick green dress that brought out her eyes and made her hair glow. Her eyes were outlined in black, and a thin gold chain drew attention to the creamy curve of her neck. She smiled as he walked in the door, her entire face lighting up. Geoffrey returned the smile, and he knew he should be thrilled to his toes that such a woman was smiling that way at him. But all he could think about was Sunny.

The evening was not nearly the refuge he had hoped it would be. Instead of distracting him from his troubles with Nash and Sunny, he spent most of the night talking about them. And when he wasn't talking about them, he was thinking about them. The need to go to Nash was almost overwhelming.

So overwhelming, in fact, that when Claire invited him back to her apartment for nightcaps, he nearly agreed. It was entirely unprofessional. It was entirely unlike him. It was a distraction, and why not indulge in some out of character behavior? Everything else was completely out of control.

Ultimately, common sense prevailed. He gently turned her down, explaining that he had an early morning, and he was feeling a little under the weather. And he was expecting a phone call from his elderly mother. The last part was a lie, and laying it on a bit too thick, but Geoffrey felt like he had to justify his decision. A simple *no thank you* wouldn't have sufficed.

He drove directly home. He didn't even entertain the notion of going to Nash's. Not seriously. Not enough to take a short detour, just to drive by his home to see if Sunny's car was there.

It wasn't.

He didn't bother turning on the lights when he returned home. He just started undressing when he walked in the back door and left a trail of clothes behind him, until he was wearing nothing but his boxers and his watch. Rubbing a weary hand over his face, he flipped on the bedroom light, and nearly had a heart attack.

Sunny was stretched out on the bed, her hands folded behind her head, her ankles crossed. She looked comfortable and composed, like she belonged in his dark bedroom, on his bed.

"What are you doing here?" Geoffrey demanded.

"I thought I'd try to talk to you, but I figured you'd try to avoid me, or run away or something. So here I am."

Geoffrey calmly reached for his robe. "Yes, here you are."

"How was your date?"

The question wasn't sarcastic. It was just a question. Like the thousands of other questions she had asked since he first hired her.

"Fine."

"I can see you're not exactly thrilled to find me here…"

"Sunny, I just need some…"

"Time? Yeah, that's what Nash said. He pretty much knew that you weren't going to come over tonight."

"Nash knows me pretty well, I guess." He saw that Sunny had no intention of vacating his bed, so he sat in the chair across the room.

"I guess so. Better than I ever could."

Geoffrey frowned. Her statement had been so simple, but full of conviction, and a bit of sadness. "You think you don't know me? You know me better than almost anybody, Sunny."

"I can't believe you never noticed."

"Noticed?"

"I barely graduated high school, Geoffrey. And I only lasted one semester in college. I thought I was going to be stuck at McDonalds for the rest of my life, or cleaning houses like my mom. I never had anything, and I never expected much. But you hired me anyway."

Geoffrey was familiar with her background. They had chosen her out of the pool of candidates because they couldn't afford to pay somebody with the qualifications they were looking for. Once they removed everybody who was out of their range, Sunny had been the best choice. Young, bright, energetic, a good attitude…

They had talked about replacing her once the business really took off. Now they could hire anybody they wanted, and Geoffrey would no more get rid of her than he would drop Nash. She did her job well.

"You had a lot of potential."

"See? You saw that. You saw something that nobody else bothered to look for. I know that Nash didn't even want to hire me."

"That's not…"

She held up her hand. "He told me all about it. How you made the final decision. Fought for me, even."

"There was a slight disagreement," Geoffrey admitted.

"But you did hire me, and it's turned my life around. So that's why I don't get it."

"Get what?"

"I don't get why you could see something that every person in my life overlooked, but you couldn't see how much I wanted you."

Geoffrey's chest tightened, and the back of his head began to throb. She sounded genuinely confused. And he supposed he didn't blame her. Because he still didn't see it. Not really. There was the kiss, the invitation, the effort of the picnic, but a part of him didn't really believe it all. He didn't know how to reply, and she kept speaking.

"But when I did everything in my power to get your attention, and you just went right on ignoring me, I thought maybe there was somebody else. Nash may not have seen it, but I did. I saw the way you watched him, like he was the only person in the world. You know when he walks into a room, it doesn't matter what you're doing, your eyes go right to him? And I figured out that maybe there was something going on there. Maybe something one-sided, but you didn't want me. That hurt."

"Sunny, I…"

"I mean, it hurt my pride. I don't want to sound like some stuck-up bitch, but that's never happened to me before."

Geoffrey wasn't surprised. Especially since, technically, it hadn't happened to her yet.

"So I felt guilty when we hooked up, me and Nash. Because I know you, and I knew it would hurt. And fuck, Geoffrey, I'm so fucking sorry. I don't know if I'd take it all back, but I think I'd like a do-over. I'd want to stop from hurting you. And now…I know you're not happy about it, but the truth is out. And you're here, and Nash's across town, and I can't help but think you're so close to finally getting what you want, and you can't have it, because I'm in the way."

"What? Sunny. No. No, that's not it. That's not the problem."

She sat up now, her dark eyes meeting his. "Nash doesn't know I'm here. I told him I was going home with a headache."

"Sunny…"

"I never stopped caring about you. And maybe that's unfair to Nash, but I care about him, too. He told me he doesn't want me to go, and I don't want to go either. But, Geoffrey, if I'm the one standing between you and the one you want, the one you've loved for ten years, then I don't have the right to stay here. It's not fair to you."

"I don't want you to leave," Geoffrey said, his words soft, his lips nearly numb with shock.

"But I think it's pretty clear that you don't want me, either."

"That's not true," Geoffrey said. Shocked silence fell in the room, and he could tell she was surprised by the strength of his denial. "That's not true," he repeated, his tone softer. "Sunny, when I hired you, I thought you would be a good addition because what you didn't know you were smart enough to learn. And I was right. At the time, I was only concerned with what you could do for us, professionally. And that's how I viewed you. As a professional…"

"Yeah, I figured that part out," Sunny said, with a hint of bitterness.

"But you didn't figure it out when I stopped seeing you as a mere colleague," Geoffrey murmured. "And I was so afraid of ruining what we had, of offending you, of scaring you away, of lawsuits, that I kept it all to myself."

"Kept what?" Sunny asked.

"I can't even look at you without wanting you," Geoffrey confessed. "Seeing you every morning is one of the best parts of my day. Maybe the best part. I love the way you smile, and I love to hear your laugh. There's actually not a single thing that I don't love about you."

Sunny stared at him like she had never seen him before. "Then what...Geoffrey..." She sighed. "I'm so confused."

Geoffrey laughed softly. "Join the club. I've been nothing but confused for the past seventy-two hours."

"So...you do want me, then?"

He smiled. "Every day."

Sunny looked at him thoughtfully. He didn't look away from her. Having her in his bedroom made him as uncomfortable as having Nash here, but it was different somehow. They both overwhelmed his senses, but Nash overwhelmed him physically, too. Sunny looked small and confused on his bed.

"I just...you're good at hiding it."

Some imp moved him to speak then. "Do you think you'd get much work done if I wasn't good at hiding it? Do you think you would feel comfortable, looking across the room and seeing me watch you? Seeing the desire in my eyes? Do you want to know how hard you make me? The things you make me think about?"

Her answer was just a whisper of air. "Yes."

He hadn't meant to go that far, and he didn't intend to take it any farther. But it was the look on her face that made him continue. Her eyes were bright, and her lips were parted. She wasn't upset by what he said, she was aroused by it. And seeing the naked arousal on her face, knowing for once that it was for *him*, was intoxicating. Overpowering. He felt a little heady.

"The cloak closet, behind my desk." Even as he spoke, he realized that Sunny and Nash might have already taken advantage of the corner of privacy. But that realization didn't come with the expected lance of pain. He didn't pause to ask about it. "I always thought I should take you out on a date. Woo you. Seduce you. Treat you properly. But sometimes, the urge to grab you, to shove you in that closet, to feel your body against mine would overcome me. It's just big enough for the two of us. There wouldn't be much room to spare."

"No, there wouldn't," she agreed, her voice tight.

"But I wouldn't need much room." He closed his eyes, bringing the image to mind, as vivid as any memory. "Because your arms and legs would be wrapped around me so tightly, and your face would be buried in my neck, your breath hot with muffled moans. I'd hitch your skirt high over your thighs, and I'd move my fingers along your thighs, feel each muscle tense as I caressed you. I'd dip my fingers beneath your panties, so I could finally feel how hot you are. So I could finally hear you moan my name. I'd slide my fingers into your pussy until you were begging me to fuck you." Geoffrey's breath hitched, and he opened his eyes to see her staring at him. Her chest was rising and falling rapidly, and a light sheen of sweat coated her forehead.

Geoffrey swallowed hard and shifted to cross his legs. In his boxers and robe, he felt particularly vulnerable, almost naked. "I think about how you might taste. I wonder what your hair smells like. I want to know how you feel when you come, and what you sound like when you want more. I want to learn every inch of your body, and watch you as you ride me until you collapse. I want to know what it's like to see you smile, and know you're smiling because of me. I think about touching you, like I have the right, like you've granted me that gift."

"Geoffrey..." She half rose off the bed, like she was going to approach him.

He put his hand up. "You need to go."

Sunny blinked and froze. "What?"

"You can't stay here. You can't...I can't... you need to go."

"Go?" Like she didn't know the word.

"Go back to Nash."

"Come with me," she said quickly.

Geoffrey shook his head. "I can't do that."

"Why not?" She exploded, clearly frustrated with the situation. "You want me. I want you. You want Nash. Nash wants you. We're all very wanting. What's the problem?"

"Are you better than human, Sunny?"

"What does that even mean?"

"Are you above jealousy? Are you above hurt? Are you above being possessive? Can you share Nash's time with somebody like me? Do you think he can share you? You guys seem to think that the three of us fucking would make things better, and it *won't*."

Sunny stood up now, but she seemed taken aback. "Not just fucking, Geoffrey. You love us both, you've admitted it."

"Maybe I only think I do."

"What does that even mean?"

Geoffrey sighed. "It means I'm not sure that sort of relationship would work for us, Sunny. It hurts me to see the two of you together. It hurts like somebody is ripping out my heart. It's a real, physical pain. How do I know that'll get better?"

"What if it hurts because you think you're excluded? What if it hurts because you think you're on the outside, looking in? You aren't, Geoffrey. You aren't, and you won't be."

"If I lost the two of you, or did anything to hurt you, or made a mess of this, it would kill me. It's bad enough to lose you to each other, but I think I can survive it. What if I lose you completely? What if it doesn't work?"

"What if you're losing us anyway because you're scared to try?"

Geoffrey felt something heavy in the pit of his stomach. The thought had occurred to him, of course.

"I should never have said anything," he murmured.

"No, no, Geoffrey," she said quickly. "That's not what I meant…"

"You should go."

"I want to work this out, Geoffrey."

"There's nothing to work out. You should go."

Sunny didn't protest a second time. She left him alone in his bedroom, feeling vulnerable and sick. And a little scared.

CHAPTER 7

Nash stared at his computer without comprehension. The black lines that should have formed words simply blurred in front of him. He knew he should be concentrating on work—and for the first time, the pressure and responsibility of being *the* boss was starting to get to him. He didn't care about work. Sunny had knocked on his door the night before, upset and almost near tears, and when he finally pried the story from her, he was at a loss of what to do, or what to say.

He wondered what he should do. What he *could* do. Wondered if maybe the only way to fix this was to get a do-over, and take a completely different course. He wouldn't change the fact that he kissed Sunny, and wouldn't change anything else he had done with Sunny since then. But he would have talked to Geoffrey about it. He wouldn't have shut Geoffrey out in some selfish attempt to keep from hurting him.

And he wouldn't have agreed with Sunny's insane plan to invite him to join them. It had seemed like a good compromise at the time, but now he could see that it only made things much worse for Geoffrey. For all of them.

But perhaps he only thought that because he couldn't *stop* thinking about Geoffrey finally saying yes. Geoffrey finally coming to his bed. Geoffrey kissing him, and stroking him, and holding him.

Geoffrey had always firmly been in the "do not fuck" category of his brain. That category was home to his brother's wife, every person Geoffrey ever dated or slept with, Sunny in the beginning, and

Geoffrey himself. Sunny had been promoted out of that category easily enough, but Geoffrey had his own little space carved out, and Nash thought that he was deeply embedded there.

It wasn't the first kiss that took Geoffrey out of the category and put him directly in the middle of the "must have as soon as possible" column. That kiss had been too rushed and too surprising to be truly stimulating—though he had certainly enjoyed the way Geoffrey kissed him back. In a way, Nash was surprised by that. He hadn't spent a great deal of time thinking of Geoffrey's mouth, but he'd never assumed the other man had so much…skill.

Even so, it wasn't the first kiss—skillful as it was—that kept Nash up all night. It was the barest hint of a kiss they'd shared the night before. It was the way Geoffrey gripped his shirt. The way he pulled Nash toward him. The way his dark blue eyes reflected his desire and his hesitation. It was a hint of what Geoffrey truly wanted to do. It was just enough to make him light-headed and ready for more.

How would things have gone if his phone hadn't rung? Would Geoffrey have stopped? Or would he have allowed that first tentative kiss to evolve into something more. Nash had been acutely aware of where they were, so close to the bed. And how Geoffrey looked, all polished and handsome for his date.

Date. Nash thought of the word bitterly. He liked Claire well enough. She was fine, as far as clients went. But what right did she have to take even more of Geoffrey's time and attention away from him? Geoffrey shouldn't have gone with her the night before, and Nash shouldn't have answered the phone. They should have let that caress lead them to wherever it was they were going.

The fact was, he wanted Geoffrey. And now that he allowed himself to admit it, instead of keeping Geoff to his proper designation—an entire designation he had created in large part *because* of Geoffrey—he couldn't stop thinking about it. There had been an element of physical attraction when they first met, though Geoffrey had seemed so far away from his type.

Geoff had been skinny. Too skinny, like nobody had bothered to feed him in days. Nash had always imagined that if he got the young man alone and naked, he'd be able to count every rib, and then maybe play them like a xylophone. He had also been shy, unassuming, and clumsy. It was the clumsiness, the running into walls, the tripping over his own feet, that baffled Nash, because when Geoffrey thought he was alone, or when he was wrapped up in something that truly fascinated him, he was a very graceful man. He wasn't a fan of sports, he didn't go out and party *any* night of the week, much less three or four nights. He didn't have a girlfriend.

He was, in short, the sort of person Nash avoided.

But he never wanted to avoid Geoffrey. In just a matter of days after they met, Nash found he was seeking out Geoffrey. And Geoff never seemed to mind the attention. Nash had always assumed that he initially welcomed Nash's company because he was lonely, and then later, when he had other friends to spend time with, he chose Nash because they were genuinely compatible.

And now Nash thought he understood. Geoffrey had always welcomed his company, always had time for him, always made room for him, followed him from job to job and then into a risky business venture because he loved him.

Nash could hardly wrap his mind around that. But it wasn't an unpleasant thought. No, far from it. It was surprising and reality shifting, but it wasn't unpleasant. It wasn't anything Nash was afraid to think about or wary to consider. He was actually happy he finally knew. Because it meant…what?

That he could finally stop keeping such a close watch on his own feelings and desires? That maybe he could allow himself to see Geoffrey as more than a close friend and business partner? Had he been waiting for that very opportunity?

Even if he accepted it without reservation, there was still the question of what he should *do* about it. He knew Geoffrey well enough to know that the initial admission had cost him dearly. Geoffrey liked to pretend he didn't have any feelings, ever, about anything. Nash didn't know if he'd call Geoffrey *repressed*, but he was certainly closed off to a degree, and very private. Nash always thought that's why he had such trouble with women. It was certainly why he'd had such a hard time with Sunny. He never expressed anything like desire, because he was probably afraid of rejection, and at the same time, he never trained himself to look for it in other people.

Nash didn't want to do anything to hurt Geoffrey. He didn't want to embarrass him. He didn't want to upset him.

But he was seeing the other man in lights and angles that he had never considered before. It was exhilarating, but also frightening. And confusing. And it made simple, routine, daily tasks seem like an effort far too great for his reserves of energy. He couldn't afford to take another day off, and he knew Sunny and Geoffrey were out in the office, pointedly ignoring each other and doing their best to work.

Geoffrey was probably steeped in his own embarrassment over his confession the night before.

It occurred to Nash again that Geoffrey needed his own office. Right now he seemed more like a subordinate than an equal. Why hadn't he noticed that before?

Nash rolled his pen through his fingers absently and examined his own office. It was spacious. Bigger than he really needed, though Geoffrey had insisted that a huge office was important for his image. Nash thought his image was just fine without the massive room. It easily took up a third of their leased space.

He stood up and began walking the perimeter, mentally building walls and moving furniture. It could easily be partitioned and made into two offices. It wouldn't take too much time or effort to build an actual wall, and in the meantime, they could put up dividers.

Nash paused at the filing cabinet, smiling softly as the memory overtook him. It was a very pleasant memory, and he never got tired of reliving it. Even if that moment might have been the starting point for all his problems with Geoffrey. Even if that moment had been the point where his life spiraled out of control. It didn't matter, because that night, at the moment their lips had touched, Nash realized that Sunny could be the woman he'd spend the rest of his life with.

*   *   *

Sunny thumbed through a thick file and grimaced. "This is a mess. Who's in charge of filing around here?"

"You," Nash answered without looking up.

Sunny beamed at him. "Oh, right. Seriously, though, boss, I think most of this is from before my time."

"Oh, I know it is. That's why we're working on it now."

"Do you ever even look at these old things?" Sunny asked. "This is from six years ago."

Nash leaned over and took the file from her hand. "We might need it one day, then won't you be happy we're doing this now, instead of springing it on you later?"

Sunny rolled her eyes. "Oh, yes, I'm so happy that I'm stuck here on a Friday night instead of doing something...you know...fun."

Nash dropped the file in the growing pile of "Things to Look at Later" and leaned against the wall. "What do you do for fun?"

Sunny shrugged. "I don't know. I like to go dancing. There are a few decent clubs around here, and it really helps me work off some excess energy. And if I don't feel like dancing, I find other ways to work off my excess energy."

"Oh really?" Nash smirked good-naturedly. "Like what?"

"Get your mind out of the gutter," Sunny admonished. "Like kick-boxing. On the weekends, I like to ride my hog."

Nash laughed now. "Your *hog*?"

"Well, it's just a little Honda, but one of these days, I'll be able to afford something a little flashier," Sunny announced, moving to sit beside him. She interlocked her fingers, resting her hands on her stomach, and smiled at him. "What would you be doing if you weren't here?"

Nash checked his watch. "Eight o'clock on a Friday night? I'd be here."

"Do you ever go home?"

"Sometimes for a change of clothes."

Sunny snorted. "You're a young guy, Nash. You should be out, having fun, chatting up the ladies, downing a few drinks."

"I do that. Well, I used to do that." Nash ran his hand through his hair and grinned at her. "Besides, you should be happy I'm such a workaholic."

"Why?"

"I sign your paychecks."

"Oh, yes, I'm thrilled that you love to work after hours and keep me here with you. I've always wanted a boss like you," Sunny teased.

"Damn right you've always wanted a boss like me. I'm a dream come true."

"Yeah," Sunny said softly, "you are."

It was the way she looked at him that made Nash understand she wasn't teasing any more. Her eyes were wide and soft, and her face was clear. There was a bold curve to her mouth, and he realized for the first time how close she actually was to him. They weren't quite touching, but they would be with little effort. Nash had never dared touch Sunny, for various reasons, but everything about her body language told him he was welcome to try.

Nash wasn't one to pass up an opportunity when it presented itself. He lifted his hand, his fingers brushing against her cheek. Her mouth parted, the tip of her tongue sliding across her bottom lip. He watched the progress of the movement with rapt eyes, and his own lips parted. He leaned forward, moving slowly but not hesitantly. He wanted to give her the chance to stop him—one more moment to take it all back—but he also wanted to trace her soft mouth with his own.

She lifted her chin, the final invitation that Nash needed. She leaned into the kiss, claiming his mouth before he had the chance to claim hers. Nash had always known she had a bold mouth from the strength of her smiles, the pureness of her laugh, the sly grins she shot him when she thought nobody was looking. But her kiss was something else entirely, something both expected and unexpected.

The initial contact was almost rough. They were suddenly hungry for each other, and clumsy in their desire. Their teeth scraped against each other's lips, and their tongues clashed, seemed to get in the way of one another. Nash didn't know what to do with his hands, and he cupped one of her cheeks, the gesture far more gentle than the kiss that was consuming them. But they weren't completely lost to it. Nash took back the reins, forcing her to slow down, to ease back.

The kiss shifted down into something far more seductive. They moved at the same time, naturally and instinctually seeking more contact. Without breaking the kiss, she pushed herself to her knees and he wrapped his arm around her, pulling her against him. She straddled him, her small hands gripping his shoulders, her breasts pressed against his chest.

Nash didn't want to stop the kiss. Not for any reason. He didn't need to breathe. If the phone rang, he would let it ring. If God himself walked through that office door, Nash would ignore him, until he had his fill of Sunny. And at that moment, Nash was pretty sure that would never happen.

When she finally did break the kiss, he almost whimpered in frustration. But he stopped, forcing himself to be an adult about the situation, and not grope at her and complain like a child until he had what he wanted again.

"Nash…"

He could have swore his name sounded different on her swollen lips. She rocked forward, grinding against his stiff cock. He was more than ready for her after only one kiss, and there was no denying it. He moaned, and she rocked again and again.

"Sunny… If you don't stop…"

"What?" she challenged.

And Nash realized she wanted him to say it. "I'm going to flip you onto the floor and fuck you until we're both walking funny."

Sunny trailed her fingers down his cheek, the simple touch igniting his skin. "Please do," she breathed.

Nash didn't have to be told twice. His cock was throbbing, and he only had one thought, one goal in mind. It was the same thought that had hovered in the back of his mind for months. The one thought he had tried to deny, to avoid, to leave behind. It was the one thought that kept him up at nights, tortured him.

He had wanted to fuck Sunny in every way imaginable since the moment they first met. He hadn't wanted to hire her because he wanted to drag her back to his bed. Geoffrey hadn't understood his reluctance, but he could hardly explain that he had very different things than answering phones in mind for her. And after he finished fucking her every way he knew how, he'd find new ways. It was an endeavor that he could easily imagine dedicating the rest of his life to.

Nash clawed at her shirt, pulling it over head, and exposing her high, firm breasts to his hands and his greedy eyes. He drank in the sight of her, converting each detail to a powerful memory. His mouth was drawn to her skin. He kissed her, licked her, teased her with his teeth, like she was a piece of ripe fruit. She continued to rock against him, a regular rhythm that did nothing except drive them both crazy.

They disposed of their clothes quickly, neither pausing or giving the situation a second thought. He pushed a stack of files out of his way, destroying the work of the past two hours, but Nash didn't care. Judging from the way Sunny arched her back and reached for him, she didn't care either.

If he was going to look for an excuse, or a place to shift blame, it would be her. Nothing she did, but rather the way she felt. Her mouth was perfect against his, as though she had been made to kiss him. Her fingers were long and graceful, and fire trailed wherever she touched him. Her skin was pale and smooth, and so responsive. She moaned at every touch, every lick, every bite, every caress. Her legs were long and graceful, and he could feel her strength as she draped her calves on his hips. Her eyes were dark and inviting, their brown depths darkening until they were almost black.

The heat of her flesh was maddening, and he could smell her arousal as he moved closer to entering her. He nudged her swollen lips with the head of his cock, and she gasped, buckling beneath him. Nash blinked several times, trying to clear his mind and his vision. She tightened around him, drawing him inside her with her legs. As his cock slid into her passage, he shuddered with pure pleasure.

"Oh...Jesus...Sunny. Oh, God," Nash gasped. His voice was

temporarily lost as they finally settled into a rhythm, but as soon as he could find the concentration to speak again, he did. "God, Sunny, I've been waiting so long to do this. You're better than I imagined. Than anything I imagined."

"I was beginning to wonder if it would ever happen," Sunny said, her fingers slipping through his hair, holding the back of his head. She brought his mouth to hers, speaking against his lips. Each word was like a fluttering kiss. "Sometimes, I just wanted to come in here, get on my knees in front of you, and suck your cock."

"Oh…Christ. Oh, Christ. I'm sorry we waited so long."

She wrapped her legs around him, drawing him deeper, holding him closer. "Me, too."

*   *   *

The guilt came later. But not much later. Just an hour, when they left the office and walked past Geoffrey's desk. They had both paused, as if they were surprised to see it. Nash had looked at the carefully kept area, noting that everything had its own place, seeing the order that reflected the organized processes of Geoffrey's brain.

Nash remembered thinking about Geoffrey's reaction then. He'd known it wouldn't be a good one, and he was still high from fucking Sunny, and they were about to go back to his place to continue where they left off. But he'd ignored the small voice that indicated it would be a bad idea, because Geoffrey would see it for what it was.

A betrayal.

Nash now knew that Sunny had had the same thoughts, but for different reasons. Regardless of what they were thinking or why, it hadn't stopped them that night. It had never stopped them.

He was being selfish. He wanted it all.

But then, that was almost his defining characteristic. He always wanted it all. More generous people called it *driven*, but he wasn't driven. He was selfish, right through his bones. Everything he did and everything he thought was always about him. He wasn't above anything to get what he set his sights on. It was why he had succeeded where so many other people had failed.

Nash returned to his desk and focused on his computer screen. The words made sense now. A lot of things made sense. The world made sense, because now he had a goal and a plan. Nothing made Nash happier than setting goals and making plans. There was a comfort to it, a recognizable rhythm and pattern.

Nash wondered if Geoffrey would realize that he was now the top priority on Nash's list.

CHAPTER 8

Sunny finished the last email for the morning with a wide smile. It had taken at least twenty minutes to write, and forty minutes before that to research in between all her other work, but the hour was worth it. She felt warm with her success the way she always did after a difficult assignment, but she didn't look to Geoff or say anything about it. She sent him a copy as well, and she would wait until he had the chance to read it.

She didn't have to wait long. She heard his computer chirp, signaling he just received a new message, and busied herself with the letters on her desk. It was a game they played, and one she would never grow tired of.

"Sunny?"

She looked up, schooling her features to hide her smile. "Yes?"

"Did you just send this to Christiansen?"

"Yes."

"Where did you get this information from?"

"The report you wrote two weeks ago." Now she frowned, the elation quickly shrinking. "Why? Is there a more current version? I didn't see one."

Geoffrey looked up. "No." He grinned wryly. "I couldn't remember. This looks great."

Her smile returned as fast as it had faded, and for a moment, there were no awkward moments, or uncomfortable memories between them. They were just sharing a moment. A moment like dozens, or even hundreds, before it. *God, I love the way he smiles.*

Maybe he could read her thoughts, because he looked away then, and the moment was lost. The tension settled over the small space again, and Sunny turned back to her correspondence. She hated this. She hated this so much, and she had nobody and nothing to blame except herself. There were maybe a thousand things she could have done differently, or she could have tried, and all of them would have kept the two of them away from this bleak silence.

Sunny watched him from beneath her lashes. She could have gawked at him openly, and he probably wouldn't have noticed. But she didn't like to openly gawk at the boss. Sunny smiled a little sadly and shook her head. Maybe if she had been a little bit more open, Geoffrey *would* have noticed, and she wouldn't have wasted over a year trying to get his attention.

She noticed that his hair was a little bit longer than he liked and made a mental note to schedule time for a hair cut. He was wearing a white shirt, which meant that his preferred shirts were all dirty. She needed to run them to the dry cleaners—she could go pick them up after work, if he didn't mind her dropping by his house. She also saw that his cup was empty. Without speaking, she disappeared into the small kitchenette and turned on his electric kettle.

Sunny didn't need to do any of these things. He never asked her to do it, and he always seemed shocked that she went to the trouble. Though she went to the trouble on a daily basis. Nash never seemed shocked, but then, Nash expected people to wait on him. He never said as much, and he never made any unreasonable demands, but she could tell he enjoyed being taken care of because he expected it.

Geoffrey enjoyed it because he never expected it.

But that didn't surprise Sunny. What surprised her was the fact that she genuinely liked taking care of the two of them. She liked making sure they were sharp and had everything they needed. She moved through the kitchenette mechanically—getting a clean mug, getting the tin of tea, taking the milk out of the small fridge. She didn't need to think to do these things; it was just part of her daily routine.

In the beginning, Sunny had worried about the way her heart skipped a beat when Geoffrey smiled at her gratefully. She had worried that a single kind or encouraging word from him would make her blood pressure skyrocket, make her face turn red. She'd never thought she was the sort of woman who needed a man's approval to feel good about herself. But almost from the first day of her employment, she cherished

Geoffrey's opinion, and was always happy when he was happy, anxious and on edge when he was not. And since she had never even liked her bosses or coworkers before, this was a startling and confusing development.

The light on the electric kettle blinked, indicating the water was done.

The mug in her hand was brown and blue. Totally plain. Nothing distinct about it, and certainly nothing that would ever catch anybody's eye. She remembered the day Geoffrey had brought it to the office. It was to replace the cup she had broken on her second day at the job. She'd been beyond mortified, especially when Geoffrey rushed into the room to make sure she wasn't hurt. She had been almost prepared to walk out the door right then and never return. But they had cleaned up the ceramic shards together, and Geoffrey had cheerfully recounted the time he had dropped an entire stack of his mother's china.

That was the first time she'd seen Geoffrey as something more than her handsome boss.

The act of making tea was almost comforting. It was her morning break, a bit of time when she got away from the endless emails and the ringing phone. But this time, it didn't make her feel better. Something like regret, and maybe fear pierced her. She didn't want to stop these little rituals, didn't want to step away from these undeniable signs that she was a part of Geoffrey's life. And she knew that if the three of them were pulling apart, if their bonds had been destroyed, she would need to leave.

While Geoffrey had always been so accessible, Nash had seemed too distant for the first year or more after she started working there. He shut himself away in his office for hours at a time, he never invited her out to lunch, he rarely spoke to her during the day except on business matters. But she was fascinated with him, all the same. Fascinated by his power, by the respect he commanded, by his easy beauty. He, like Geoffrey, was a new sort of specimen in her life, and she studied him with the same devotion that she had for Geoff. But she had never even dared to hope that he felt anything for her.

Until he kissed her.

Sunny replaced the milk and pulled a bagel from the fridge. She popped it into the microwave for a few seconds, until it softened, and then smeared it with cream cheese. She was worried that Geoffrey wasn't eating. She had no proof either way, except she knew that he forgot to feed himself when he was under particular stress. The past few days were pretty damned stressful, in her opinion, and she honestly wouldn't be surprised if the last meal he had was their ill-fated picnic.

Sunny grimaced at the thought. At the time, it had seemed like a good idea. Definitely something worth trying. But in her own excitement, and greed, she had forgotten what she really *knew* about Geoffrey.

For example, he didn't like surprises.

Sunny wanted to apologize for that, but Geoffrey would probably misunderstand and think she was apologizing for the *offer*. And she most certainly did not want to take *that* back. Especially after his confession the night before. She was a little bit obsessed with it.

With tea and bagel in hand, she returned to the front office, and silently set her offering on his desk. He dragged his eyes away from the computer long enough to notice. "What's this?"

"Your breakfast."

"I…" He looked from the food to her and smiled. It was just a small smile, but it was genuine. "Thanks. Sometimes I think you can read my mind."

Sunny almost laughed. If the past few days had taught her anything, it was that she didn't know Geoffrey nearly as well as she thought she did.

"Just doing my job," Sunny said before sauntering back to her desk.

God, she loved the way he smiled. She really, really did.

She needed to fix this.

She had no idea how to fix this.

The last time she'd attempted to fix things, she'd made everything worse. The events of the day before were on a regular loop in her mind, but she was trying not to wallow. She couldn't get any work done if she spent too much time thinking about the way he had kissed her, the things he had said to her. Like he loved her.

Geoffrey *loved* her. *Her.* She'd be walking around with a goofy smile if everything else wasn't so fucked up.

Maybe she could think of some excuse for him to come over. Or for him to drive her somewhere. But she didn't have any emergencies, and she knew that adding a deception on top of everything else wouldn't endear her to him. Or worse, he would suggest she ask Nash for help.

Sunny tapped her teeth with her fingernail, staring at Geoffrey thoughtfully. She supposed it was just as well that he didn't want to talk to her. She wouldn't get any work done if he wasn't ignoring her, because she sure as hell wasn't ignoring him. How many times had he thought about taking her into the closet? How she wished she could have found a way to let him know that she wanted it, too.

She shifted in her seat, warmed by the thought. If she didn't rein herself in soon, she'd be wet and utterly distracted.

Sunny turned back to the computer and opened her email. Maybe Nash would help.

* * *

Geoffrey had never been so acutely aware of another person's presence in his life. Even the times when Nash would crash in his dorm room, and he'd lay awake all night listening to the other man breathe wasn't as distracting as this. He heard every sigh, saw every movement out of the corner of his eye, and could even feel her watching him. It had been a relief when she finally went into the kitchenette, but the problems only intensified when she returned with his tea and bagel.

And why was she fetching him breakfast? He had told her and told her that it wasn't necessary, but she never seemed to pay him any attention.

He snuck a glance her way and saw that she was staring at the computer with what looked like a smile and a frown. Her eyes were serious, but the corners of her mouth were upturned slightly.

It was utter torment. A torture devised by some sadistic god. Maybe Cupid was real, and he was currently fluttering behind Geoffrey's shoulder, laughing at the merry mess he had just made. And there was no sign that this torment was ever going to end. Not unless one of them left, and the thought pained him. They were stuck.

He leaned back in his chair and rubbed his eyes, exhausted after his sleepless night and busy morning. When he opened his eyes again, Sunny was standing next to his desk. He frowned, surprised. He hadn't even heard her get up, and her chair squeaked every time she moved. She was smiling and there was a too bright gleam in her eye.

"What?" he asked.

Sunny answered by folding her fingers around his and squeezing his hand. The unexpected contact was like a punch to his midsection—it didn't hurt, it just stole his breath from him. He nearly pulled his hand away, but the contact was too pleasant. He didn't want to lose it just yet, selfishly hording every second he could get from her.

She pulled him to his feet, and he opened his mouth to protest. He didn't know what she needed or wanted from him, but he had work to do. And he was trying to concentrate and behave like everything was the same between them, and he couldn't do that if she insisted on touching him.

"I've been thinking," she said slowly, backing toward the wall, pulling him with her. "About everything. What you said last night. What I wanted to say to you. The way I need you."

"Sunny, now isn't the time…"

"I think it is, Geoff." Sunny was against the wall now, and she tugged on his arm, slamming his chest against hers. She wrapped her other arm around his back, securing him in place. "I can't think of anything better to be doing right now."

Geoffrey opened his mouth to protest, prepared to cite every client, every assignment, every chore and errand that needed to be done for the day, for the week, for the month. But she took advantage of his parted lips with a deep kiss. He froze as soon her lips touched his, and jolted back to life when her tongue brushed against his. Her arm tightened around him, and her breasts strained against his chest—they seemed to beg him for attention. Her mouth was coaxing, the kiss slow and generous, and it didn't give him a single inch. She was taking from him, and trying to draw more, and it was all so deliberate, so thorough. Geoffrey couldn't withstand it, and he melted into the kiss, responding in kind.

As soon as he shifted his response, she reached behind her and pulled the closet door open. Geoffrey was aware of that, but barely aware of what she had in mind. Before he could respond, she pulled him inside and slammed the door behind them.

"What are you doing?" Geoffrey said, trying to reach the knob. She stepped between him and the door, blocking it.

"What we should have done a long time ago," Sunny answered, sliding her hands over his shoulders and down his back.

The closet was dark and small, and in the tiny space, he was more aware of her than ever. A brief surge of panic overtook him. He couldn't withstand her and he knew it. If she kissed him again, he'd give in. And he couldn't give in. He couldn't let things go that far. It was one thing to admit his desires and feelings—though painful in its own right—it was quite another to show her. To demonstrate it. To be stripped and vulnerable, until there was nothing shielding his heart from her.

"What about Nash?" Geoffrey murmured. "I told you last night…"

She stepped aside, as much as she could, and allowed him to try the door. It was locked. He couldn't see her face in the dark, but he knew that she wouldn't be surprised by this development. They were conspiring against him, again.

"This isn't a game, Geoffrey," Sunny said softly, her voice almost tangible in the dark. "I'm not trying to play with you. Or to hurt you. I don't want you to be upset with me, or ignore me. I don't want you to be scared."

Geoffrey's throat felt tight. "Sunny."

She put her hand on the back of his neck, her fingertips playing with the fine hairs there. She guided his mouth toward her, pausing with less than an inch separating their lips. Her breath was like a caress on his mouth, hot and warm and smelling vaguely of her coffee. "I've been waiting to do this for a very long time, Geoffrey."

It was her words, more than the sudden hungry pressure of her mouth, that made him hard, made him eager to close the little bit of space between them. His first inclination was to doubt her, doubt what she said, look for an ulterior motive to this entire situation. But she was being honest with him and he knew it. He could hear it in her voice and, more importantly, he could feel it in the way she kissed him, in the curve of her body as she held herself against him.

Geoffrey buried his hands in her hair and returned the kiss, his tongue sweeping into her mouth. She made a sound of satisfaction. And everything was caught up in a blur. Whatever doubts he had about the situation were suddenly gone, as was anything that resembled reason or logic. His hunger, unsated for far too long, took over, piloting every move, directing every thought.

He had rehearsed this moment in his mind so many times that his hands knew what to do. He pulled at her blouse, breaking the kiss only long enough to yank it over her head. He moaned softly at the first brush of her skin against his fingers, and she echoed that sound as he finally cupped her breasts, sliding his palms along her hardening nipples. She arched toward him, her mouth finding his again and, for a moment, everything fell away.

*   *   *

Nash looked at the closed and locked door with curiosity, a bit of relief, and above all, lust. He could easily hear them. And he imagined their bodies coming together, their limbs entwining, their hungry mouths seeking each other again and again. He knew the way Sunny would look, her legs wrapped around Geoffrey's waist, her face buried in his neck, so she could muffle her screams of pleasure and lick the salt from his skin. More than that, he knew how she would feel.

He locked the front door of the office, sat in Geoffrey's chair, just feet away from the closet, and unzipped his pants. His cock was hard and slick, and the last thing he wanted was to feel his own hand. It was easy enough to imagine himself in Geoffrey's place. He closed his eyes, and suddenly, Sunny was on his lap, her body electric, moving and writhing against his. Her breasts were soft and full against his chest, her thighs were slick with her arousal, and her hair was rich against his face and shoulders. He had her body committed to his memory, and he was in no danger of ever losing it.

But he found his mind drawn to Geoffrey again and again. How did Geoffrey look when he completely turned himself over to his base desires? How did he move his body when he was seeking more contact, more heat, more of everything? Nash wanted to rip that closet door open and watch, find out, have all his questions, and then some, answered. But he understood that Geoffrey needed the privacy. They needed to move slow with him. As slow as they could, at any rate.

There was a loud thump and then two distinct moans. Nash whimpered, his fingers tightening around his shaft.

*   *   *

Geoffrey's mind was gone. He could easily find a dozen *good* reasons to stop, and maybe another two dozen less-convincing but still sound reasons, if he was willing to make the effort. But once he had her skirt pulled high over her hips, and his fingers between her thighs, pushing her arousal soaked panties out of the way, his brain took a vacation. All higher-order thinking, everything that separated men from animals, had simply disappeared. In its place was a honed hunger, something pointed and desperate, and it felt so good even as it tied his stomach in knots.

He pushed the thin material of her thong aside and slid his fingers along her swollen lips until he found her clit. She bucked against his hand, his name escaping her lips in a whimper. He was fascinated with the way she felt. He had never touched anything so soft, so alluring, so hot and ready. Her clit jumped against his finger each time he caressed the throbbing flesh, and she jerked against his hand each time he applied a bit of pressure, so wonderfully, instantly responsive.

Geoffrey knew he didn't have time to do everything he wanted to do. He was disappointed by that until she unzipped his pants and wrapped her fingers around his cock. Then all thoughts of exploration, of extending it, of torturing her, and by extension himself, fled. They didn't exist. Nothing existed except his need to be inside her, his need to be surrounded by her completely.

He pulled his fingers away and brought them to his mouth, his cock jerking at the first taste of her. His blood was humming in his ears and his skin felt tight, stretched over his flesh, and electric. His clothes were too tight, irritating his flushed, sensitive skin. The only thing that would sooth it would be to strip and slide his body along Sunny's, but he didn't have that option.

"Geoffrey...I want you..." Sunny said, stroking his shaft, then sliding the heel of her hand over his head, smearing the pre-come found there. "Right now."

His muscles tightened as a shiver raced down his spine. It felt like she had just touched him with a cattle prod, sending multiple volts of electricity coursing through him. He slid his hands along her ass and lifted her feet off the floor, giving her the chance to wrap her legs around him. There might have been a second of hesitation, but that seemed entirely inconsequential as she kissed him again. The sensitive tip of his cock slid against her lips and, finally, he thrust deep into her pussy, slamming her back against the wall.

"Geoffrey..."

Geoffrey struggled to breathe, his chest constricting even as she tightened around him. It was so much like he always imagined it would be, and yet, nothing at all like he had pictured. He couldn't have known how she would really feel, couldn't have known how her hair smelled, couldn't have known how she would claw his shoulders, grasping for a hold, even as she slammed down on his cock.

"Oh...Sunny..." Geoffrey gasped. "Oh, fuck."

Her mouth was near his ear, and he could hear the smile in her voice. "I'm trying."

All too soon, Geoffrey could feel the pressure building, feel his balls tightening. A part of him was unreasonably convinced that *this was it*. He'd never get another chance to be with Sunny again, never get another chance to experience this level of bliss. Every cell in his body seemed to be crying out for hers, and every inch of him was hot, glowing, suffused with pleasure. His regret at being dressed was acute, a sharp pang. And he tried to resist. He tried to resist her perfection, the release she offered, the relief he longed for.

Geoffrey tried to hold himself back, but he couldn't. Momentarily forgetting where they were, even who he was, he shouted her name as he came, his body tensing deep inside of her. Aftershocks rolled through him, his hips jerking involuntarily with each one, until finally he was still and the only sound was his ragged gasps and her harsher breathing.

After several seconds, he began to get feeling back in his legs, and his head began to clear. He realized she was still clinging to him, and still waiting. His face grew hot again, but this time it wasn't with need or passion, but rather, embarrassment. She would compare him to her other lovers—to Nash—and find him wanting.

Hoping to salvage the situation, he reached between their bodies and found her clit. Her flesh jumped beneath his touch, and she moaned, encouraging him to continue. His cock was still semi-erect, and as she clenched and thrust against him, he began to harden once again. She lifted her head, and in the dim light, he could barely see her face, but he saw her lips, parted and swollen from his kisses. His mouth found hers as he pinched her clit between his forefinger and thumb, and she shouted his name into his mouth, the vibrations moving down his neck.

Geoffrey knew he could probably go for another round, but then they would never leave the closet. He would just keep fucking her, and he would never have enough. Now that the initial fog of lust was beginning to evaporate, he was beginning to remember himself, remember where they were, remembered why they shouldn't be there at all.

With a great effort, he separated their bodies, pulling free from her tight muscles, and setting her feet on the floor. She sort of slumped there for a few minutes, supporting her weight against the door. The space suddenly seemed very cramped. He needed to get out of here, needed to get a drink, and the chance to breathe. Needed to wash the smell of their sweat and sex from his hands before it drove him crazy.

He reached for the doorknob, rattling it fruitlessly, and she covered his hand with hers.

"Geoffrey..."

"Sunny."

"I..."

He cut her off quickly. "I need some air."

"What? Oh. I..." She knocked on the door with her other fist. Within seconds, Geoffrey heard the lock click.

The door swung open slowly to reveal Nash standing there, his arms crossed, an unreadable expression on his face. Geoffrey felt like a child, caught in the middle of some criminal act, and about to stand trial in front of judge, jury, and executioner.

Nash and Sunny exchanged a glance, and then Sunny fluttered by them. Geoffrey wanted to follow her.

"I think we need to talk," Nash murmured. "Privately."

"I have to…"

"Now."

It wasn't a tone that Nash took often with him because it didn't fit. Geoffrey wasn't his subordinate or his child, and he did not appreciate being ordered around. He never had. The first time Nash had tried it, like Geoffrey was nothing more than his lackey, Geoffrey had made it clear that the second time would result in very uncomfortable consequences.

This time he followed Nash into his office without comment.

CHAPTER 9

Nash leaned against his desk, his legs stretched in front of him, his arms folded across his chest. Geoffrey remained near the door, though Nash had pointedly gestured at the chair beside him. A quick escape might be necessary, and Geoffrey wanted to be prepared for that. The last of his post-sex high had lifted as soon as the door shut behind them, and now the silence was stretching like bitter taffy between them.

Geoffrey didn't know what to say, so he waited. He couldn't read Nash, and that disturbed him more than anything Nash could actually say. He could still smell Sunny, still smell their mingled bodies and sweat. The scent of their coupling hung around him like a cloud, and he thought that Nash probably couldn't smell it from across the room, but he was still self-conscious.

The silence started to make him itch, and that life-long impulse to head trouble off before it could start overtook him. He opened his mouth to apologize—he couldn't do anything else. How could he explain? Of course, a part of him recognized that an apology wasn't necessary. Wasn't it Nash who'd locked the closet door? Who'd unlocked it?

The phone rang. And rang. Nash ignored it. Seconds later, his cell rang. He ignored that as well. It occurred to Geoffrey that they had to get this shit sorted out, and fast, because it was affecting their business.

"Nash…"

"Geoffrey…"

They spoke at once, then both fell silent. It was the sound of Nash's single word that stopped Geoffrey. He sounded confused, like he wasn't even sure what Geoffrey was doing there. Geoffrey thought his face probably reflected Nash's confusion. What was one supposed to do in this situation? Geoffrey had never thought to prepare for it.

"I need a drink," Nash murmured.

Geoffrey nodded, foregoing his canned lecture on drinking during office hours. He had a policy about fucking coworkers during office hours, too, but clearly they were throwing policies and rules out the window for the day. He could hear Sunny moving on the other side of the door. She was no doubt curious, straining her ears to every word, yet pretending she wasn't. Geoffrey was half-tempted to just open the door so she could see them standing there, staring at each other like fools.

Nash poured two drinks from his secret stash that Geoffrey always pretended to be ignorant of, then downed his without further hesitation. Geoffrey couldn't help but watch as he swallowed, noting the movement of his throat and the way his jaw clenched when the strong whiskey hit his stomach.

"That was harder than I thought," he finally said.

"I'm sorry," Geoffrey said, the words that had been held at bay now flying out.

Nash looked confused. "No, not...you. I just...this is crazy."

Geoffrey smiled slightly. "Yes, well, now you can understand what I was trying to say." Geoffrey handed his full glass back to Nash with a slight nod. Nash downed that, too. Once it was gone, Geoffrey felt a twinge of regret—he needed it more than he thought.

"If you had told me last month...hell, even last week...that I'd be in this position, I would have laughed and suggested you hand over your drugs."

Geoffrey frowned. "Nash, I don't quite follow."

"I was listening," Nash admitted. It didn't come as a great surprise to Geoffrey, so he merely nodded and encouraged him to continue. "And I was...imagining...what was going on. And you were all I could think about."

"Oh." Geoffrey didn't know what he should say to that, what *could* be said to that. He didn't know what it meant, either.

"Come over to my place tonight," Nash said, almost like he was asking.

Geoffrey nodded. He couldn't hide from the situation, and they couldn't very well continue their nearly silent staring contest. "Yeah."

"I'll order something for dinner."

"Okay." Geoffrey reached for the door.

"I was thinking just the two of us."

Geoffrey looked over his shoulder, his eyes meeting Nash's. Something seemed to pass between them, something powerful enough to make the back of Geoffrey's neck tingle. He nodded and then slipped out of the office.

Sunny was sitting behind her desk, looking cool and professional. A remarkable feat and, he realized, a necessary trick when you're fucking your boss literally behind your other boss's back. Geoffrey dismissed the bitter thought, shocked at himself for even allowing it to pass through his mind.

Sunny calmly finished her phone call, logged the appropriate information into her computer, and then turned to look at him with bright eyes.

"We're going to discuss it after work," Geoffrey said before she could ask.

"Discuss?"

Geoffrey shrugged.

"You know I don't mind the two of you…talking, right? As much as you need to."

Geoffrey sighed. "Why, Sunny? What are you getting from this?"

She smirked. "Isn't that obvious?"

Geoffrey refused to rise to her bait. "No."

Her smirk faded and she nodded. "My serious answer? You two are the most important people in my world. The only people I really even care about. I was being selfish with Nash, and maybe I'm being even more selfish now, but I want you both. I want to be with both of you. I care about you both…I care about you just as much as I care about him."

Geoffrey looked down, suddenly very interested in his desk. After a few seconds, the phone rang, and the day resumed as though nothing had interrupted it.

*   *   *

Nash's apartment was kept meticulously clean. His maid, Sally, came in three times a week, but he never left a mess for her to clean up. He vacuumed, scrubbed and put away his dishes, dusted, and mopped the kitchen floor every night. As far as Geoffrey knew, Nash had always been this way. Geoffrey found the familiar smell of lemon soap and the familiar sound of the vacuum deeply comforting as he let himself in Nash's apartment.

The promised food was waiting for them in the small kitchen— several Styrofoam boxes from Nash's favorite Chinese restaurant. There was a six-pack of beer in the fridge and a pink box full of chocolate chip cookies that Sally probably bought that morning. He helped himself to one and opened a beer, trying to pretend that this was like any other time he dropped in after work.

The vacuum cut off and seconds later, Nash entered the kitchen.

"I thought I heard you come in," he said, walking to the fridge.

"These are good cookies," Geoffrey said, pushing the box toward him.

"You're going to spoil your dinner."

Geoffrey shrugged. He didn't have much of an appetite anyway. How could he even think about food in a situation like this? Nash didn't seem perturbed, though. He pulled two plates from the cupboard and began to heap them with food. Geoffrey didn't comment, just watched the growing mountain of fried rice, noodles, and orange chicken.

He followed Nash to the table, sitting in his regular seat. With a start of surprise, he realized he *had* a regular seat. And the beer in Nash's fridge was Geoffrey's preference. Even the cookies were more along his tastes than Nash's. And he didn't think Nash planned it that way, or went out of his way to stock up for Geoffrey's regular visits and meals there. That was just the way it was.

Sometimes he wondered why they had ever stopped living together. Geoffrey knew what his logic was at the time—he was an adult with a good income and he should have his own place. Plus, he hated to watch Nash and his never-ending parade of dates. But every once in awhile, like now, he remembered just how comfortable he had been as an almost constant part of Nash's life.

"You need to eat," Nash said, gesturing toward Geoffrey's untouched plate. "We haven't done this in awhile, have we?"

"No, not since...well, it's been a little over a month, hasn't it?" Geoffrey didn't mean for the question to be sharp, but Nash looked guilty anyway. Geoffrey sighed. "I'm sorry. I didn't mean that to come out the way it did."

"No, it's okay. You're right."

"I'm being childish."

"I don't think I'd behave much better if I were in your shoes," Nash admitted softly.

"You are." Geoffrey shrugged. "In a way."

"No. What happened today between you and Sunny wasn't a surprise…or a betrayal."

Geoffrey pushed his food aside, hoping that now he could give up the pretense of caring about dinner. "What were you trying to tell me today?"

"I was hoping we could get through the meal first," Nash said wryly.

"It's been driving me to distraction all day."

Nash leaned back in his chair and dropped his fork. "Yeah, me, too. But probably for different reasons."

"Probably for the same reason," Geoffrey corrected.

"Our first place was smaller than this room, wasn't it?" Nash asked conversationally.

Geoffrey looked up, surprised by the parallel to his own thoughts. "If it wasn't smaller, it wasn't much bigger either."

"We practically lived right on top of each other."

Geoffrey nodded. "Yeah, I remember."

"Sleeping in the same room every night, sharing a bathroom, pooling our money for beer and smokes. I thought we didn't have a single secret between us."

Geoffrey stiffened. "If you're suggesting I ever did *anything* that was inappropriate…"

Nash shook his head quickly. "No, I'm not. And that's just the thing, Geoff. I don't understand how we could be so close for so long, and I just never knew. I keep thinking about it. Either you're a great actor, or I'm the biggest jerk on the planet."

"Can't it be a little of both?" Geoffrey asked with a smile.

"It probably is," Nash acknowledged. "I've also been thinking a lot about missed chances, about things I could have done, should have done, differently. You may never have done anything to tip your hand, but there were…openings. There were times I could have acted."

"And you wish you had?"

"Yeah."

"Why?"

"Because I liked the way you kissed me."

"Oh. And you…want to make up for lost time now?" The question was more curious than hopeful.

Nash nodded.

Geoffrey's stomach dropped like a stone. He reached for his beer, hoping the cool liquid would help sooth the sudden dryness of his tongue. Nash silently watched him drink, and his eyes seemed riveted to Geoffrey's mouth as he licked the drops of beer from his lips.

"Do you?"

Geoffrey blinked, surprised that the question even had to be asked. But then, Nash had extended such an invitation before, and Geoffrey had done everything he could to get away from the issue.

"Nash..." Now seemed the time for open honesty, and Geoffrey tried to brace himself for the fallout. "This isn't...this isn't a game to me. This isn't something I can just do on a lark. It's...it'll hurt me too much."

"What will?"

"If you wake up tomorrow morning and decide this was all a mistake."

"That won't happen."

"How do I know that?"

"Because I'm asking you to trust me."

Geoffrey swallowed. It was as simple as that. All he had to do was trust their friendship, trust Nash's word, as he always had.

"You do trust me, don't you?"

"Of course."

Nash smiled. The smile that stopped Geoffrey's heart in his chest. It was rare, that smile. And perfect. He'd smiled that way when he landed his first job after they graduated, and again when they opened the doors of their own firm. It was the smile Geoffrey had seen when he opened Nash's door and saw him with Sunny. It was the smile that Geoffrey had always coveted.

"I was hoping you'd say that."

"You should have already known the answer."

"My modesty kept me from being certain."

Now what? The question was unformed, but Nash must have seen it in his eyes. He stood and reached for Geoffrey's hand, pulling him to his feet. Geoff didn't resist. There was still the memory of doubt in the back of his mind, still a sting of apprehension, and the tumble of nerves in his stomach, but he didn't resist.

Geoffrey knew what to expect now. Knew how Nash's lips would feel when they finally brushed against his. Knew to expect Nash's tongue to invade his mouth, knew to tilt his head up slightly instead of down, knew that Nash's chest would be solid, and his grip hard. He knew what to expect rationally, because he had relived their two brief kisses over and over, savoring every detail.

But he didn't know what to expect at all.

The first kiss had been a shock, too surprising to really savor. The second kiss had been too brief. Both kisses had them holding something back. Even now, Geoffrey could feel himself holding back, not pushing too hard, or going too far. But Nash didn't have any such reservations. He unleashed himself, pouring so much into the kiss that it overloaded Geoffrey's mind.

He gripped Nash's shoulders, bracing himself, and responded in kind. If Nash was going to be unreserved, then Geoffrey wasn't going to hold back, either. Their lips seemed sealed together, their tongues moving sinuously against each other, their teeth clashing. The force behind it pushed Geoffrey backward, until he was against the wall, crushed between it and Nash's hard body. He could feel Nash's cock against his thigh, feel his erection even through his thick jeans.

They were finally forced apart, both in desperate need for oxygen. Their gazes locked as they gasped for air, and Geoffrey realized the kiss had probably shattered the last of his defenses. He had no doubt that every emotion, every moment of need, every fantasy and passionate thought was currently reflected in his eyes for Nash to see. He had layers and layers of shields, endless walls, and that kiss had demolished them all, leaving him entirely vulnerable to the man standing just inches from him.

Nash scrutinized him for a moment, and then tilted his head, bringing his lips to Geoffrey's once again. And once again, Geoff thought he knew what to expect. He was prepared for another onslaught, another attack against his senses, but this kiss was something else entirely. His lips were slightly swollen and bruised, and much more sensitive, and his body was crying out for more contact, his hands already seeking any bare bit of skin he could find. The slow, gentle, silky kiss didn't alleviate any of the pressure, but it did catch him off guard.

He moaned into the kiss, stepping forward to press his body completely against Nash's. Not a single inch separated them, and even through the material of their clothes, Geoffrey could feel the heat rolling off Nash's body, feel the echo of Nash's heart against his chest. The first kiss had been frantic and a little frightening in its hunger, but this kiss was much more subtle. Geoffrey felt like he could stand here, like this, pressed between Nash and the wall, and kiss him for hours.

He wanted to explore every nuance of Nash's mouth. He wanted to learn all its textures, all the sensitive points, all its secrets and crevices.

The kiss broke in stages, as though neither of them could bear the thought of ending it. Each time one would pull away, the other moved with him, until they were reduced to taking small sips of air before claiming another kiss. Geoffrey didn't know if it was Nash, or the lack of oxygen, that seemed to make the ceiling spin above him, but he didn't really care. He just gripped Nash harder and moved in closer.

Nash was the first to pull back completely, his face flushed and his eyes bright. Geoffrey tried to resist, but Nash leaned back, out of his reach. Geoff self-consciously brushed his lips with the back of his hand, wondering if he would ever be able to get this hunger under control now that the dam had been breached.

"Where did you learn to kiss like that?" Nash asked, his voice a little shaky. "I mean…damn."

"I was just following your lead."

Nash looked skeptical. "Maybe you have more of a private life than I gave you credit for."

Geoffrey snorted. "You gave me credit for having a private life?"

"I figure you've got to do something to fill those long winter nights." Nash tilted his head toward the door to the hallway. "Do you want to…?"

Geoffrey nodded. "Very much."

Nash bestowed that rare and wonderful smile on him. "Good, because I've been thinking about you all damned day."

Geoffrey arched his brow. "Oh really? Maybe I should make you cool your heels for a few weeks, let me show you what it's like."

"You wouldn't."

"How do you know?"

Nash slid his hand down Geoffrey's body to brush against the bulge in his pants. It was just a moment of contact, but it made Geoffrey gasp, a wave of heat flooding his body. "Because you're as ready as I am."

Geoffrey considered replying, letting the easy banter continue, but it seemed a pointless thing to do. It was just a sign of his nerves, of that curious combination of terror and anticipation. They were on the edge of a line, a line he was more than prepared to cross, but he couldn't see what, if anything, was on the other side. It seemed like the past decade had been leading to this moment, and Geoffrey hadn't done anything to prepare himself for it.

He nodded and released Nash. There was a long pause before Nash finally stepped back, freeing him. Geoffrey silently followed the other man out of the kitchen, turning the light off behind him, and realizing with a small start that Nash was leaving a mess on the table. Leaving it like it didn't even matter, like the thought of it wouldn't drive him crazy. Geoffrey thought about pointing it out, but decided if Nash didn't care, then he wouldn't worry about it either.

Nash's bedroom was spacious, and his huge bed dominated the room. Geoffrey had never really allowed himself to think too much about the fact that the mattress was more than big enough to accommodate both of them. But now he couldn't stop seeing the two of them stretched out, naked, skin wet and glistening, Nash's body sliding over his, the heat surrounding him like a thick blanket, as Nash finally…

Geoffrey shivered, everything from his throat to his balls constricting. He realized at that moment he was going to lose control. He was already barely holding on to his composure with a fingernail, but as soon as he could see, touch, and taste Nash's body the way he had always dreamed about, he was going to completely lose it. The realization frightened him. He didn't like to be out of control. He didn't like to let his body, or his mind, run away from him. He didn't want to surrender that last part of himself to Nash, turn everything he was over to Nash completely.

"Is there something wrong?" Nash asked quietly.

Geoffrey looked up, pulled from his thoughts, and met Nash's eyes. They were a warm brown that reminded Geoff of melted chocolate. Suddenly, those concerns evaporated, unable to withstand the warmth and intensity of Nash's gaze. What did it matter if he completely lost control in Nash's bed?

Geoffrey trusted him, after all.

"Nothing wrong at all," he murmured, reaching for Nash. None of his fantasies had ever worked out quite this way. He couldn't quite put his finger on the difference between expectation and reality, but it was no less real, no less apparent. He was a lot less certain of himself, of his abilities, of his decisions. And, if it was possible, he was more attuned to Nash and the way he reacted. As Geoffrey began to unbutton Nash's shirt, he was painfully aware of each brush of skin, each breath, each flicker of pleasure in Nash's eyes.

Geoffrey made short work of the buttons, his mouth set in a grim line as he concentrated on the task. He sucked his breath in sharply as he pushed the shirt down Nash's shoulders, exposing his muscled chest.

It wasn't the first time Geoffrey had seen his bare chest—or stared at him—but it was the first time he could give into the impulse to touch him.

Nash sighed softly as Geoffrey dragged his fingertips down his chest to his navel. His muscle twitched under Geoffrey's touch, coming to life like Geoffrey was shocking him. Geoffrey knew that Nash didn't have the time he once had to exercise, but that didn't mean he was slacking off either. His muscles were defined and hard, his skin stretched taut, a golden brown. His chest had a slight covering of hair, and a thin line that moved down his stomach. Geoffrey traced it now with a shiver of pleasure.

"Geoffrey…" It was a soft moan, like he wanted more and yet was perfectly satisfied with what he had.

Geoffrey's mouth watered as he looked at Nash's unblemished skin. Without warning, he leaned over and dragged his tongue over a dusky nipple. Nash gasped, the sound going straight to Geoffrey's groin. Geoff gripped Nash's hip, pulling him closer, and began to explore Nash's chest with his mouth. He circled one nipple with his tongue, pulled the other between his teeth, kissed a trail along the top of his ribs, and sampled the salty skin at the hollow of his throat.

He could feel it happening now, the steady loss of control. He needed so much of Nash, needed to fulfill so many desires, needed to put to rest so many questions. He was still fully dressed, his cock heavy with desire, his stomach moving in a continuous circle, and despite the pain of his situation, he could have been happy to simply touch, lick, and kiss Nash for the rest of the night.

"I want to feel you, too, Geoff."

Nash's request was soft, yet firm. Geoffrey stepped back and lifted his T-shirt over his head, waiting patiently while Nash devoured him with his eyes. It was like Nash had never seen him before, like they had only just met, and this was Nash's only chance to commit each inch of him to memory. Geoffrey didn't have any self-conscious urge to turn away or distract Nash's attention. He was already completely exposed emotionally, after all. Geoffrey remained still as Nash reached for his buckle, working it free, before slowly pulling down the zipper. The pants slipped from Geoffrey's slim hips and his boxers soon followed.

Geoffrey could almost feel the weight of Nash's gaze he looked at his exposed and erect cock. "Have you…done this before?"

Nash looked up. "Yeah."

"I never knew."

"Have you?"

"Yeah."

"I guess we're both pretty good at keeping secrets."

Geoffrey could only nod. He hadn't revealed the full truth—or even most of the truth. Every time he'd had sex with another man, it had always been in a moment of keen desperation, when his need for Nash had finally eclipsed his ability to satisfy himself. He wondered if Nash had a specific type, a specific need he tried to meet.

And then he had a more unsettling thought. Was it possible he didn't know Nash nearly as well as he thought he did? Nash had been having regular sex with Sunny for the past month, and he'd never suspected. Nash had apparently been having sex with men, and Geoffrey not only never suspected, he'd been convinced Nash was actually as straight as a man could be.

Before Geoffrey could pursue that line of thought further, Nash wrapped his fingers around his shaft and stroked his flesh. Geoffrey's legs seemed to turn to water, and he swayed forward, bracing himself on Nash's shoulder. He somehow found the presence of mind to unzip Nash's pants and push them down, and finally, they were both naked.

The weight of the thought almost knocked Geoffrey off his feet again. He was standing in Nash's bedroom, naked, leaning against Nash's body, his cock dripping with pre-come, his balls already tight, and his pants in a heap around his ankles. "Oh, my God," he murmured, not meaning to speak at all.

"What?"

"I just…" With a great effort, he took a step back, forcing Nash to drop his hand. "This. Us. What we're doing."

"Do you not want to do this?"

"No, I do," Geoffrey said quickly. "But…"

"No," Nash said quickly, invading Geoffrey's personal space again. "No buts." He took Geoffrey's wrist and guided his hand to his shaft. "I'm so hard for you…"

Geoffrey didn't hear anything else Nash said. His blood was rushing in his ears, and he was completely engrossed with the way Nash felt. Like the kiss they shared, this was an experience Geoffrey wanted to savor. He realized that he had so many things he wanted to do, so many things he wanted to try, that he would need much more than a single night to accomplish it all.

Nash groaned and gripped Geoffrey's arms, pulling him closer while simultaneously stumbling toward the bed. They fell backward on the mattress, Nash bracing himself at the last moment to keep from crushing Geoffrey beneath him. Geoff didn't mind in the slightest. In fact, he welcomed the pressure of Nash's weight pinning him to the bed. He wrapped his free arm around Nash's back, holding the larger man against him as he continued to stroke his cock. The tip dragged against his belly, leaving a sticky line of pre-come.

Geoffrey's oldest and best fantasy struck him then with such force that he nearly whimpered. The desire to act out that fantasy was like a physical hunger—his stomach clenched, his mouth watered, his spine tingled. It didn't help that Nash had discovered the very small, sensitive spot just below his ear, and was now biting and licking with such ferocity that Geoffrey was actually squirming beneath him like an over-excited puppy.

"You're so sensitive," Nash murmured, and Geoffrey shivered from the puff of warm breath. "Are you this sensitive everywhere?"

Before Geoffrey could answer, Nash was drawing his fingers up the side of his ribs. He moved like he was searching for something, and the second he found it, Geoffrey realize he *was* searching for something. He jumped at the contact, but it wasn't ticklish. Not necessarily. It wasn't entirely pleasant either, though it was far from painful. Geoffrey didn't know what it was, except that no lover had found it before, and no lover had touched him like that before.

"Nash, I want…"

Nash shook his head slightly and moved down Geoffrey's body, stopping any hint of further speech. Geoffrey decided it was just as well. He had been on the verge of spilling every single secret desire he ever harbored. With half-closed eyes, he watched Nash's dark head as he moved lower and lower, licking and nibbling and sucking and kissing as he went. Geoffrey moaned and arched off the bed, squirming and reaching for him. *How does he manage to find so many of these magic little spots?*

It gradually occurred to Geoffrey that Nash wasn't finding heretofore unknown spots. When it came to Nash, Geoff's entire body was one giant, pulsing nerve-ending. It didn't matter how he touched him, or where he touched him, only that he *did* touch him.

Nash's mouth moved lower and lower, following its own invisible path, until his lips were so close to the base that Geoffrey could feel each breath of air against the tight skin of his cock. He held his breath, trembling, and wondered if he should tell Nash—ask Nash for what he wanted.

"Nash..."

"Hmm?" He slid his tongue along the inner-curve of Geoffrey's thigh, and Geoffrey temporarily forgot what he was going to say. Every tendon from his thighs to his stomach tightened, and he arched his head back, unable to breathe until Nash finally removed his tongue. "You were going to say something?"

"I..." Geoffrey relaxed against the bed again. "God, Nash, I want you to suck my cock." The words came out in a rush of breath, and he lifted his head slightly so he could look at Nash. Their eyes clashed for a moment before Nash ran his tongue along the bottom of his cock, tracing the line from his balls to his slit, gathering a string of sticky fluid as he went. Geoffrey sighed raggedly, his head falling back.

It was clear Nash had done this sort of thing before. He moved without hesitation or question, his long tongue circling the head before he drew the full length of Geoffrey's cock into his mouth. Geoffrey shuddered as he brushed the back of Nash's throat, his hips jerking, his hands clutching the bed reflexively. The evidence of Nash's experience sent a sharp stab of jealousy through him. It was an entirely different feeling than when he pictured Nash and Sunny together. Nash and Sunny was understandable. But Nash sucking another man's cock, possibly at the exact minute Geoffrey had been fantasizing about that very thing? The thought was maddening.

Maddening, but ultimately pointless. And it was stupid to dwell on it, because Nash wasn't with another man now. Nash was kneeling before him, his hands gripping Geoffrey's thighs, his mouth impossibly hot and soft, his tongue clever and intoxicating. And the sounds he made—the soft grunts and groans from the back of his throat—were unlike anything Geoffrey had ever imagined. The hungry sounds were almost addicting because he never knew Nash was capable of making them.

Geoffrey reached down with one hand, running his fingers through Nash's dark hair. It felt almost like silk as each hair tickled his fingertips. He sought out Nash's skin, caressing his ear, his neck, his cheek, his touch both hesitant and insistent.

He remained more or less coherent, capable of logical thought, and even speaking if he had to, until Nash relaxed his throat and swallowed him completely, his lips wrapped tight around the base of his cock.

"Oh...oh fuck...oh yes...oh..." The words lost shape completely, dissolving into moans. As Nash began to move, wrapping his strong fingers around Geoffrey's shaft and stroking him firmly with each upward motion, Geoffrey's eyes rolled into the back of his head, and the moans turned to shouts. He was distantly aware of the fact that he was making a great deal of noise, but he was entirely incapable of doing anything about it. It seemed like if he didn't give voice to his pleasure, somehow vent the unbelievable satisfaction bubbling inside of him, he would shatter. Break, somehow.

The explosion, when it came, happened without warning. One second, Geoffrey was straining toward Nash, awash in sensations he didn't have names for, and the next, he was coming so hard he could feel it in his fingers and toes. Nash paused as Geoffrey's jizz hit the back of his throat, but he didn't pull away. He swallowed every drop, and then licked his shaft and head clean, teasing the too-sensitive skin until Geoffrey was panting, begging him to stop.

When Nash finally did cease his attack, Geoffrey didn't know if he should be grateful or not. He closed his eyes, counting each breath as his pulse slowed, and waited for Nash to stretch out beside him. But the seconds passed and he remained alone. He head felt hot, his throat sore, and he knew his satisfaction would only be temporary. The moment he opened his eyes to see Nash's nude body, he would no doubt be ready for another round.

The mattress shifted beneath Nash's weight, and Geoffrey opened his eyes. Nash was already wearing a condom, and he was holding a tube of lubricant. Geoffrey sat up, startled. A part of him had known things would go this direction, a part of him had hoped, but he still didn't quite expect it. He had been with other men before, but he had never let another man fuck him.

Nash might have seen the surprise on his face, because he paused and looked a little uncertain. "Is this okay?"

It was a simple enough question, but Geoffrey's mind froze. It wasn't that he didn't want Nash. He most certainly did. And he wanted Nash any way Nash wanted him. He nodded.

"Have you ever done this before?"

"No."

"But I thought you said you've been with other men?"

Geoffrey's words were hoarse, his throat still sore. "Not like that."

Nash stretched beside him, his skin oddly cool against Geoffrey's. He dipped his head and teased Geoffrey's lips with his tongue before slowly probing Geoff's mouth, deepening the kiss by degrees. Geoffrey could taste his own come on Nash's lips and tongue, and he found that deeply erotic and exciting. His cock stirred, and he surrendered to the kiss completely. He sensed Nash moving, heard him squeeze lube from the bottle onto his finger.

Geoffrey lifted his knees, pushing his ass off the mattress. He could feel Nash smile against his lips, and the startling cold gel against his skin as Nash sought his tight ring of muscle. Nash's finger slid into him easily, and Geoffrey tensed at the initial intrusion, surprised by the way it felt, but not uncomfortable. Nash continued distracting him with his mouth, kissing him thoroughly as he pumped his wrist.

Once Geoffrey relaxed, Nash slid a second finger into Geoffrey's passage, pushing up to the third knuckle. Again, Geoffrey tensed, trying to deal with the unfamiliar, but not quite unpleasant sensation. A different sort of feeling than before overwhelmed him. It made him feel like his limbs weren't quite attached to his body, like his brain wasn't quite getting enough blood, like he was going to start screaming again. It occurred to him that if he continued reacting like this, he'd lose it by the time Nash used a third finger.

"Does that feel good?" Nash asked.

"I...I don't know."

"Does it hurt?"

"No."

"Are you ready for more?"

Yes, no, and always. Geoffrey nodded mutely, but almost cried out in protest when Nash pulled his hand away completely. He broke the kiss long enough to cover his fingers with lube once again, and then slowly pushed three fingers past Geoffrey's pucker, stretching and filling him. Geoffrey began to pant, struggling for every bit of air, every fresh breath. The ceiling tilted above him, and a subtle ache spread through his groin, his lower stomach, and down his thighs. It wasn't painful, but it was very insistent.

"Are you ready for me, Geoffrey?" Nash's mouth was near his ear, and his voice was so low and rich, spreading like honey.

Geoffrey nodded. "I am," he gasped. He wanted to add more. Like how much he wanted him, how much he *always* wanted him, how long he had been waiting for this moment, and now that it was there, how he didn't know quite what to think or what to do.

Nash pulled his hand away, leaving Geoffrey feeling oddly empty. He positioned himself between Geoffrey's legs, forcing his knees up until Geoffrey was spread before him, open, welcoming, wanting. His cock and balls were heavy, his ass slick, and his breathing labored. Nash studied him with half-closed eyes, like an ancient god judging the offered sacrifice.

Nash spread more lube on his cock, coating the condom, and then guided himself forward. Geoffrey held his breath, but tried to relax. He knew that if he was tense, this experience would be more painful than pleasant. For both of them. He felt the head of Nash's cock nudge his ass, and experienced a brief flare of panic. Nash was too big. This was never going to work. This was going to *hurt*, and he didn't know what to do about it.

But when he looked at Nash, his apprehensions didn't seem to matter. Nash's eyes were dilated, and it seemed there wasn't a hint of color in his dark eyes. His mouth was partly open, and his chest was moving rapidly, like he was struggling to get enough air, too. Geoffrey was glad that Nash had insisted he turn over. He wanted to see this, wanted to witness every second, every expression on Nash's face.

Nash moved slowly, carefully. It was an eternity of heartbeats, of moans, of gasps. It was golden pleasure with veins of red pain. It was impossible for Geoffrey to close his eyes, and impossible to keep them open. It was some sort of spiritual awakening, and it was completely, wantonly physical. It was an unknown need sated. When Nash was finally fully seated, his cock completely sheathed in Geoffrey, they both paused, grasped blindly for each other, held on tightly. Geoffrey had never felt closer to another person in his life. He hoped Nash was feeling the same thing, hoped this all wasn't just one-sided.

"Oh, my God, Geoffrey," Nash groaned. "So tight...and hot....God..."

Geoffrey felt a little bit like Nash could split him apart, but he had been careful when preparing him, and the pain was minimal.

When Nash finally started moving, pulling out slightly and then corkscrewing his hips as he thrust forward again, Geoffrey couldn't hold himself back. All of his fears about losing control had been completely right and totally baseless. He was right that he *was* going to lose control, but there was nothing to fear. It was all right. He could turn his body over to Nash without hesitation. And he didn't have much of a choice, because his brain was shutting down, too overwhelmed by the pure, simple *pleasure* moving through his body in ripples that grew to waves.

Nash leaned forward and kissed him, catching Geoffrey's shouts with his mouth. Geoffrey tried to move with Nash's body, tried to match his rhythm, but he felt mostly like he was squirming and flopping. He needed to move, but he wasn't doing so very gracefully.

Nash didn't seem to mind. The kiss was almost violent, Nash's tongue fucking his mouth, but Geoffrey responded in kind. Every feeling, every response, was heightened and distorted. He was just a pile of quivering, naked, needy flesh, operating without the benefit of higher brain functions.

But Nash surprised Geoffrey. As the rhythm of his hips shifted, grew more frantic, as his cock moved in and out of Geoffrey's body with more ease, the kiss changed. It no longer matched Nash's thrusts. Geoffrey's cock slid against Nash's stomach, the sensitive head brushing against his hip, and Geoffrey would have begged Nash to touch him, but Nash fisted his shaft before Geoffrey had to say a word. He could feel his second orgasm rushing forward, especially when Nash shifted and began hitting his prostate with every thrust.

Nash lifted his head, breaking the kiss, and as soon as Geoffrey's lips were free, he could feel the beginning of a shout bubbling at the back of his throat. But the sound was stilled when his vision cleared and he got a good look at Nash's face.

Everything froze. Geoffrey had never seen that expression on Nash's face, that peculiar light in his eyes. But it didn't matter if it was unfamiliar, it wasn't unknown. It was an open look, honest, completely without pretensions or shields. Geoffrey could only stare, both understanding and not understanding.

Nash loved him. That was love shining in his eyes.

He didn't have to say a word. He may never have to say a word. Geoffrey *knew*, the same way he knew his own name, the same way he knew that the sun would rise in the morning. He felt weak, like everything inside of him had melted, and he clung tighter to Nash, closing his eyes and wrapping his arms and legs around the other man.

"Open your eyes, Geoff," Nash commanded softly. When Geoffrey complied, Nash kissed him. "Come for me. I want to watch while you come for me."

Geoffrey barely heard his soft command, too caught up in what he was seeing on Nash's face. And he realized it was the sort of naked emotion he had seen from Nash before, and had never been brave enough to name it, and now he knew, and his hips jerked forward. He never closed his eyes or looked away as the orgasm crashed through him, his come coating Nash's stomach, and then sliding against his own skin as Nash shifted and thrust deeper.

"God, Geoff," Nash choked out before his body tightened. Geoffrey could feel him shaking and trembling, his orgasm echoing through his muscles. "God."

But he didn't pull away, even after they were both spent, exhausted, slick with come and sweat. Geoffrey was still struggling for breath when Nash kissed him, and he completely forgot that he even needed oxygen. His legs and arms were tight around Nash, and grew tighter still as Nash deepened the kiss. Nash had never kissed him like this— he used his entire body, rocking slightly against Geoff, building the friction between them, his tongue clever and searching, and the softest moans of desire that Geoff didn't so much hear as he felt. They vibrated from Nash's chest and through him. Geoffrey kissed him back with as much honesty, following Nash's lead, not holding anything back.

Eventually, they were forced to separate as Nash slipped out of him. He stood, moving to discard the condom and grab a towel to wipe them both clean. Geoffrey couldn't do anything except watch, unable to speak. But even if he had the capacity for it, he didn't know what he could say. What needed to be said?

Nash stretched out on the bed beside him, and surprised Geoffrey by pulling him against his side. Geoffrey relaxed against him, realizing that Nash liked the close contact. He buried his face in his lover's neck, inhaling the scent of his aftershave and salty skin, completely content.

"Geoffrey?"

"Hmm?"

"That was really…"

"Yeah."

"Are you okay?"

"Fine."

"Maybe we should shower."

"Let me rest for a minute here."

"Maybe we should shower after a nap."

Geoffrey nodded, his tongue darting out to taste Nash's skin. "That sounds like a good plan."

Nash squeezed him briefly, then relaxed. His breathing evened, then matched Geoffrey's, and soon, they were both dozing.

CHAPTER 10

Geoffrey hung in limbo for several minutes, drifting out of his dreams and back into the waking world. He slowly became aware of the fact that he was not alone. Something hot and solid was pressed against his back, a heavy arm draped over his ribs. He had no idea what time it was, no idea how long he had been asleep, and for a few long seconds, no idea who he was with.

The person stirred behind him—*Nash*. He was with Nash. Now his body remembered with his mind, and he realized he was still a little sticky, still a little sore, and still very satisfied. He needed that shower. More than that, he needed to turn around and confirm with his eyes what his body and heart already knew. Slowly, so as not to disturb the sleeping man behind him, he rolled to his other side and opened his eyes.

He needn't have worried about waking Nash. He was awake, looking at Geoff with heavy-lidded eyes.

"I thought you were going to sleep through the weekend," Nash said.

"I haven't been sleeping well."

"Insomnia again?"

"Again? It never really goes away." Geoffrey smiled. "Except now, I suppose."

Nash dipped his head and kissed the corner of his mouth. "How 'bout that shower now?"

Geoffrey nodded, but he wasn't in any hurry to get out of bed. On the other hand, getting out of bed in order to join Nash in the shower was pretty strong incentive. He untangled his legs from Nash's and stiffly crawled out of bed. He was more tender than he initially thought.

"I think that's a bit more...exercise than I'm accustomed to," Geoffrey murmured, stretching his legs.

"Maybe we should do what we can to get you accustomed to it," Nash suggested.

"I think that might not be a bad idea," Geoffrey agreed.

They stumbled into the bathroom together, their minds still stinging with lethargy, their bodies uncoordinated. But Geoffrey felt better as soon as the hot sting of the water hit his neck and back. Nash's shower was spacious with strong pressure, and Geoffrey knew from experience, a large water-heater. They could probably spend an hour in there, and as soon as Geoffrey saw Nash's body glistening beneath the spray, he didn't want to be anywhere else.

Nash grabbed the bar of soap first and began creating a thick lather. Within seconds, his hands were covered in foam, and he was reaching for Geoff with a small smile. Before Geoff could speak, or even really think, Nash was spreading his hands over Geoffrey's shoulder, chest, stomach, and then his groin. Nash's soapy fingers found his cock, and he began stroking Geoffrey's shaft with both hands, pulling first one palm, then the other, down the hardening flesh. Geoffrey's knees buckled. Hissing, he grabbed for Nash, steadying himself against the other man as he continued his steady, slow pace.

"Nash...please...I'm too sensitive."

"I just want to make sure you're clean," Nash pointed out reasonably.

"I am...I am..."

Nash stopped, but Geoffrey's relief was short-lived. "Everywhere?" he asked, sliding his hand down to Geoffrey's balls, and then behind his sac.

Geoffrey sucked his breath in sharply, widening his stance. Nash tormented him with his fingers, sliding the tips along his sensitive skin, teasing him, stroking him with just enough pressure to make the floor tilt beneath him. This was dangerous in the slick shower, where his footing wasn't exactly sure, but Nash didn't seem the least concerned about that.

"Your skin's so soft," Nash murmured, his words almost lost beneath the roar of the shower.

Geoffrey tried to wipe the water from his face with one hand, the other still gripping Nash's arm tightly. He realized that Nash had no intention of stopping any time soon, content to fondle and rub Geoffrey's balls with his slick hands, occasionally applying pressure, but mostly just running his fingers over him. Geoffrey reached for the soap, resolved to fight fire with fire.

Nash gasped, seemingly surprised as Geoffrey ran the flat of his palm, now covered in soap, up the top of Nash's shaft. He ran his hand down again, moving his wrist in a circular motion as he reached the sensitive skin of the head. Nash tensed, his hand momentarily stilling on Geoffrey's body. Geoff continued to move deliberately, seeking to torture and torment him until he was begging Geoffrey to stop.

"Geoffrey...oh, God...Geoff...you're going to kill me."

Geoffrey smirked. "I'm sure it's not that bad."

"Oh, God...fuck...not bad...good."

Geoffrey looked down and studied Nash, allowing himself the chance to really *look* at him without fear of reprisal. After all, you never want to get caught gawking at another man in the locker room, and Geoffrey especially never wanted to get caught gawking at Nash. But now he was free to look as much as he wanted, and he was intent to take advantage of the opportunity.

Nash's cock was long and thick, a vein running along the top of his shaft. He wasn't freakishly huge, but he was nicely endowed, and Geoffrey loved the way it felt in his hands. He also loved the way it felt inside of him. He slid one hand down to cup his balls, noting that they were heavy, the skin smooth because of the heat, and judging from Nash's sudden quickening of breath, sensitive. His other hand gripped the base of Nash's cock, brushing against the nest of curls there.

Looking and rubbing was fun, but Geoffrey knew that he wanted to fulfill all his fantasies. He stepped aside, allowing the pulsing water to rinse the soap from Nash's skin, and then gripped the other man's hips as he lowered himself to his knees. The water poured down Geoffrey's face and made it difficult for him to see. But he didn't need to see—not once the tip of his tongue found Nash's head, sampling the hot, sweet-smelling skin.

Nash slid his fingers through Geoffrey's hair, resting his palm on the top of his head. Geoffrey ignored him, and Nash didn't try to push for anything more than Geoffrey was trying to give. Geoff circled Nash's head with his tongue several times, delighting in the texture, the taste, and the way Nash sounded each time he caressed his glans. He waited until Nash's patience was nearly gone. His first sign was the way Nash thrust his hips forward. The second was when Nash's hand tightened on his scalp.

Geoffrey relaxed his jaw and throat, calling on the memory of all his other experiences to guide him now. Every time he went down on another man, a part of him considered it practice. He'd never truly thought he'd be in this position with Nash, but if that day had ever arrived, he'd wanted to do it right.

He wanted to make Nash beg and whimper and moan. He wanted Nash to not only enjoy the experience, but crave it—crave *him*—later.

Geoffrey guided Nash's cock into his mouth, his fingers curled around the base to hold him steady. Once Nash was fully enveloped by his mouth, he used his other hand to lift the weight of Nash's sac. He rolled his balls between his fingers, and began to bob his head. Each stroke and thrust was measured, slow, and designed to prolong the experience as long as possible. Nash's hand began to flex and relax on his scalp, a thoughtless, automatic reaction, and his hips began to move in a steady rhythm.

Geoffrey started to hum. He could feel the vibrations roll from his tongue and the roof of his mouth to Nash's cock. It wasn't long until all Geoffrey's actions were working in tandem. The rhythm of his head as he moved up and down Nash's cock, the slow movement of his tongue as it twined around Nash's shaft and head, the vibrations coming from his lips, the ever-so-slight pressure from his teeth on each downward stroke, and the dance of his fingers over and around Nash's balls.

"Fuck...oh fuck, Geoffrey...oh, Geoffrey...fuck...fuck yes like that. Oh, like that. God, don't stop. Don't stop, Geoffrey. *Please.* Oh fuck."

Geoffrey couldn't help but smile at the hurried moans and pleas. Each word turned Geoffrey's insides to a warm goo, made his hard cock twitch with need, made him ache. This was what he had wanted for so long, and getting the chance now, and knowing he was doing it *right*, made the wait worth it.

"Geoffrey...I'm going to..."

It was all the warning Geoffrey got before Nash stiffened and pushed his hips forward once more, the head of his cock sliding into Geoffrey's throat. Nash convulsed, his cock jerking, and came deep in Geoffrey's mouth, forcing him to swallow the salty liquid. Geoffrey did so without hesitation, his muscles tightening around Nash again and again until there wasn't anything left to swallow.

Nash pulled away slowly, moaning and wincing at the slow slide of

Geoffrey's tongue along the underside of his spent cock.

"Jesus, Geoff…" He grabbed Geoffrey's arms, pulling him to his feet. Without another word, he smashed his mouth against Geoffrey's lips, his tongue invading Geoffrey's mouth. Geoffrey wrapped his arms around him and kissed him until his lungs ached and his lips were swollen.

*   *   *

They ate a very late dinner, or a very early breakfast. Geoffrey didn't know which. All he knew was that the left-over takeout seemed oddly appealing, and he was starving. He couldn't remember the last time he had been so hungry. His stomach was a big, hollow void in the middle of his body, and once he was finished with his meal, he felt like he could happily eat more.

Nash must have shared his appetite, because as soon as he was done with his noodles and orange chicken, he was scavenging in the fridge for more. Geoffrey leaned back in his chair and watched, appreciating Nash's naked body in the light of the fridge.

"If I had known I'd work up this sort of appetite, I would have stopped at the store after work," Nash said ruefully as he set turkey, cheese, and mayonnaise on the counter beside him.

"A sandwich sounds just about perfect right now," Geoffrey said.

"Good, because that's all I have to offer."

"This all doesn't quite seem real to me yet."

Nash wiped his lips with the back of his hand—they looked about as swollen as Geoffrey's felt. "It's real."

They both jumped as the phone rang, and Geoffrey glanced at the digital clock on the microwave, annoyed. "Who could be calling at this hour?"

The phone was shrill in the darkness, and their eyes met as one word tumbled out of their mouths at the same time. "Sunny."

Abandoning his sandwich, Nash hurried to find his phone. From the living room, Geoffrey heard him answer. "Hey."

The thought of Sunny came with a pang of guilt, but Geoffrey realized it wasn't because he had just spent the entire night fucking her boyfriend. The guilt was a result of something else entirely. His behavior that afternoon had been appalling, and she deserved an apology. She deserved the best apology he could imagine.

The conversation was short. Nash returned a few minutes later and retrieved his sandwich. "She wanted to know if you were here. If we had worked out our issues."

"What did you tell her?"

"I told her we were doing fine."

Geoffrey nodded, frowning slightly.

"We are doing fine, aren't we?" Nash asked.

"What? Oh, yes. I was just..."

"Worried?"

"How did you know?"

Nash took a big bite of his sandwich. "You're always worried about something."

"This afternoon...shouldn't have happened..."

"I don't know. I think it was a good idea. I thought you enjoyed yourself."

Geoffrey shook his head. "No, I did. But that's not how...that wasn't how I wanted our...first time to be. I shouldn't have done that. I treated her terribly."

Nash chewed thoughtfully. "And now you want to make it up to her?"

"I'd like to. If I could." Geoffrey grimaced. "I've made such a mess of things, I don't even know if that's possible. I'd like to take her out tomorrow night."

"Just the two of you?" Nash asked.

"If you don't mind."

Nash shook his head. "No, no, I think that would be good for the two of you."

"Nash...is this what we're doing now? The three of us? Working together, sleeping together, going out together?"

"I...I guess so."

"I'd like you to be certain."

"I think it can work, Geoff. If we all want it to. And if we're honest."

"I want it to," Geoffrey admitted softly.

"Then there you go."

Geoffrey stood and carried his plate over to the sink. "I think we should set some ground rules."

"You always think we should have ground rules. God, you made me sign a contract when we first moved in together. Remember that?"

"And you were glad you did it, if I remember correctly," Geoffrey countered. "I just like to have everything laid out, so there are no surprises."

"Why don't you bring Sunny by tomorrow after your big date, and we'll get everything…laid out?" Nash suggested.

Geoffrey smirked. "Why do I have a feeling that there's going to be very little talking?"

"There will be talking," Nash protested. "Eventually."

"I suppose that's all I can ask for."

Nash stood and approached him, cornering him against the sink. "Oh, it's not *all* you can ask for."

Nash dipped his head and kissed Geoffrey, his hands braced against the counter on either side of Geoff. Geoffrey responded immediately, greedy for more, as though he wouldn't get another chance to kiss his new lover. All thoughts of ground rules and serious discussions and future considerations fell away as he wrapped his arms around Nash and deepened the kiss.

*   *   *

The only person that could convince Geoffrey to get out of Nash's bed was Sunny. If he wanted to do this right, he needed to get up early and get to work. And that meant leaving the warm curve of Nash's body, the pillow redolent with his soap, and shampoo, and aftershave, the expensive silk sheets warmed by his body. Nash tried to pull him back to the rumpled blankets, but Geoffrey resisted.

"I've got to go," he protested.

"So early?" Nash muttered.

"Yeah. I've got to take care of some stuff first."

"So early?"

"It's not really that early, Nash."

"Late night…" Nash's hand curled around his wrist.

"We did have a late night," Geoffrey agreed. On impulse, Geoffrey lifted Nash's hand to his mouth. "We'll come by tonight. I promise."

"Tonight? This afternoon."

"Tonight."

"Humph." Nash pulled his hand back and rolled onto his side. Geoffrey took a moment to admire his strong back, resisting the urge to reach out and run his fingers down Nash's spine. He knew that if he touched Nash's firm skin, he'd be forced to caress him, and then kiss him, and then crawl back into bed with him.

Which would be counterproductive.

Nash started snoring again, and Geoffrey could only smile. Turning away from the bed, and temptation, he began to gather his clothes. He already knew what he was going to do for Sunny. He thought the plan was a good one; he hoped Sunny liked it, too. He was nervous.

It was ridiculous to be so nervous. Hadn't he already been through the hard part? It didn't happen the way he would have liked, but the sex with Sunny had been incredible. And now he knew where he stood with Nash, knew that this wasn't some game, knew that they wanted him. There was no reason to be nervous. No reason to already feel a little sick to his stomach.

Except this was a test.

Could he and Sunny have a normal, comfortable date? Could they spend the day together without both of them wishing they were with Nash instead? And later, could they come back to Nash's apartment and...

He'd think about that when it happened. In the meantime, he could only focus on one thing at a time. And right now, that was getting ready for Sunny.

Geoffrey let himself out of the apartment quietly, locking the door behind him. He'd left Nash's in the early morning hours countless times before, but he almost felt self-conscious now. It didn't matter. Nobody saw him.

He was home and in the shower by seven, and was dressed and ready to meet Sunny by eight. He dialed her number, and she answered after the first ring.

"Are you still at Nash's?" she asked, by way of greeting.

"No, I came home to shower and change."

"Oh, I was thinking about you two all night."

"I'm sorry."

Sunny laughed. "Don't be. I'm not. It was very...pleasant."

"Yes, it was pleasant for me, too. Have you got plans for this morning?"

"I was going to paint my toenails and do some laundry."

"Well, that does sound awfully important..."

"It can wait," Sunny cut in. "What have you got in mind?"

"A picnic."

"A picnic? Haven't we already tried that?"

"We did, but I think I ruined it," Geoffrey said.

"You didn't ruin it."

"Let me make it up to you."

Sunny hesitated a moment. "Just you and me?"

"That's what I was thinking."

"Can you give me an hour to get ready?"

Geoffrey smiled widely. "I'll see you in one hour."

"I can't wait."

CHAPTER 11

Sunny would never admit as much, but she had been holding the phone, willing it to ring, when Geoffrey called her. She had spent a long, sleepless night thinking about Geoff and Nash, and she hadn't lied. It wasn't unpleasant to think about. But it was worrisome. She didn't think she was jealous, but she was a little scared.

Geoffrey had wanted Nash for *years*. And Nash had been eager to be with Geoffrey. What if they decided at some point in the night that they didn't really need her? What if Nash called her and told her he wanted to break things off? And that would ruin everything. She couldn't continue to work for them. Hell, she might not be able to remain in the state. And a part of her had just known that the phone call was coming.

Geoffrey inviting her on a picnic was such an unexpected, welcome, wonderful turn of events. Her heart was still hammering in her ears as she surveyed her closet, looking for just the right outfit. She had tried to dress for him before and always thought it didn't have an effect on him. Now she knew that it had always affected him; he was just very good at hiding it.

She hoped they were done hiding. She hoped things were different now. She strongly suspected that most of Geoffrey's insecurity stemmed from his feelings for Nash. She *hoped* most of his insecurities stemmed from his, until now, unrequited feelings for Nash. She couldn't understand why a man like Geoffrey would have such low self-esteem.

After several minutes of consideration, Sunny chose a short denim skirt and a black baby-doll T-shirt. She wanted Geoff. And she wanted him to be unable to resist her. She smiled to herself. After that performance in the closet, she didn't think she'd ever have to worry about Geoffrey resisting her again.

She was ready with just about five minutes to spare. She checked her hair and make-up obsessively, looking for the smallest flaw. She changed her shoes four times, even though she knew Geoffrey wouldn't notice her footwear at all. Sunny couldn't remember the last time she'd been so nervous about a date. Even when she and Nash had gone to pick up Geoff, she hadn't been this nervous.

Sunny was standing in front of the hall mirror, debating whether or not to wear her hair up when he rang the bell. As soon as she opened the door, she forgot about everything else. She even forgot about the planned picnic. She had never seen Geoffrey looking so good. And it wasn't just his clothes—though his white shirt was sharp and his blue jeans appropriately tight. There was something in his eyes, something about his smile, that made her heart beat in triple-time.

Geoffrey looked happy. Genuinely happy. And satisfied. And confident.

She had always been attracted to Geoffrey, but now she was enthralled by him.

"Hey," he greeted, holding out his hand.

She smiled in returned, shyly taking his hand. He pulled her against him, and she lifted her chin, welcoming his lips. She expected his kiss to reflect the gleam in his eyes, but he was surprisingly gentle, even chaste. The kiss wasn't enough to get her pulse racing, but the promise behind the kiss nearly made her feel faint.

"Ready?" he breathed against her lips.

Oh, yes. Yes, yes, yes. Instead of dragging him into her bedroom, she nodded. "I'm set."

"Great." His grip was tight around her hand, his fingers dry and soft. Her lips were still tingling from the caress, and her face felt flushed.

"I'm surprised you wanted to meet so early," Sunny commented, trying to find her equilibrium.

"Oh?"

"Well, Nash sounded a bit…tired…when I talked to him last night."

Geoffrey smiled at that, like he was holding a secret he wanted to share. "He's probably still asleep."

"Probably," Sunny agreed. "I just thought you'd want to…spend some more time with him."

"I want to spend some time with you, Sunny."

Sunny wasn't surprised to hear him say that, just like the kiss didn't surprise her. But again, it was the promise behind the words. It was something sinful and playful and alien. She didn't know what to make of it, but she liked it.

He escorted her to the car, holding the passenger door open for her. He released her hand as she settled inside, and she felt a pang of regret at the loss of contact. It was going to be very difficult keeping her hands to herself, and she hoped they were going to a semi-private place. It wouldn't be fair to expect her not to touch him at all when he was looking and sounding and even smelling so delicious. She couldn't help but inhale deeply as he slid into the driver's seat.

"Can you tell me what happened last night?"

"Do you want details?" The question was playful, like maybe he would give her the details if she asked.

"Yes."

Geoffrey smiled. It sent delightful chills down her spine. "We can give you the details later, if you'd like."

"I'm curious about how close reality matches fantasy."

"From experience, I can tell you it's better."

Sunny laughed and ran her fingers along his jaw. It was an experimental touch, just to see what he would do. He didn't pull away from her, didn't try to put more space between them. He hadn't shaved that morning, and the stubble was rough, yet alluring, against her skin. She traced the line of his jaw to his ear, and then moved her fingers down his neck. He tilted his head slightly, in invitation.

"Are we going to the botanical gardens?" Sunny asked.

"Actually, no. I was able to find something a bit more private."

Sunny shivered again. "Oh, really? Where?"

"A friend of mine is the manager of a rather large green house. It's not open to the public, so I thought it would give us a little privacy."

"Or we could just go back to your place," Sunny suggested, encouraged by the mention of privacy.

"That wouldn't be a proper date, would it?"

"Do we need to have a proper date?" Her fingertips drifted over his shoulder and down his chest. His skin was so warm through his thin shirt, and he tensed slightly beneath her touch. "I thought we were beyond that now."

"We got ahead of that, but now we're going back to it," Geoffrey explained.

Sunny frowned thoughtfully. "Why?"

Geoffrey didn't seem perturbed by her question. "Because," he explained patiently, "I wanted you, and I wanted…that to happen. That's always going to be true, and I don't regret what we did. But I regret the way it happened. You deserve better."

"It was pretty damn good," Sunny assured him. She was touched by his gesture, but not surprised. "But…thank you."

"I treated you horribly yesterday."

Sunny frowned. "No, you didn't."

"I barely even talked to you."

"Geoffrey…" Sunny leaned back in her chair, trying to think of the best way to phrase what she wanted to say. She didn't want to upset or offend him, but she did want him to know that he didn't have to keep up the constant self-recrimination. "Geoffrey, you are harder on yourself than you deserve. You always think the worst of yourself, and I don't understand why. There's probably a good reason for it, probably somebody hurt you. But you don't need to spend your life apologizing to me for every little slight, real or imagined."

"Sunny, I'm just…"

"I know." She cut him off. She was on a roll now, and she wasn't ready to stop. "I know, you just want to make sure I'm happy, that you do this right. But, Geoffrey, can't you see? You're not going to upset me, or hurt me, or…anything because this is what I want, this is what I've been waiting for. I love you and…"

They both froze as the unexpected words hung in the air between them. Sunny hadn't had any intention at all to tell Geoff she loved him, but now that she had, she realized that she'd been waiting to say it for a very long time. And she was happy she finally told him. Happy and relieved. Now he knew exactly where she stood, and where he stood, and that was good.

"You…" The car slowed to a stop. He faced her. "You love me?"

"Yeah. Yeah, I do."

"I…you always manage to knock me off-center, Sunny."

"I think that's why you love me."

"That's not the only reason."

"Now can we go back to your place?"

Geoffrey smirked. "No."

"Now you're just trying to torture me."

"Is it working?"

"Geoffrey, I haven't been waiting for years for you to take me out to brunch. We've eaten together several times," Sunny pointed out in her most reasonable voice.

"Yeah, but I spent all morning getting this brunch ready."

Sunny could tell when she was beaten. Geoffrey clearly didn't intend to budge on this issue. All she wanted to do was straddle his lap, lick the strong line of his jaw, and hold on tight as he thrust into her. She didn't think she was asking too much, especially since she knew for a fact that he wanted her to do just that.

"So...did you fuck Nash?" The question was casual, and though she didn't think it was really any of her business, she liked the way he sputtered and blushed.

"Sunny."

"What?"

"Can you warn me before you ask questions like that?"

"I'm just curious."

"What do you think?"

"Hmmm." Sunny twirled her fingers through her hair as she considered Geoffrey's question. It would have been impossible to answer with any degree of certainty if she was basing her decision purely on what she'd witnessed in the office. Nash was naturally the alpha-male, but he never actually treated Geoffrey as a subordinate. They always seemed to be on equal footing. On the other hand, based on her experience in bed with Nash, she knew he liked to be in control.

"I think you both got a blowjob, and he fucked you. At a minimum."

He looked at her curiously. "Did Nash tell you that?"

"No. Why? Am I right?"

"I'd rather talk about you and me right now."

"I'd rather do more than talk," Sunny countered.

"You're an impatient girl."

Sunny gaped at him. "I'm impatient? *I'm* impatient? I have been waiting for you for years."

"Then a few more hours won't kill you." He parked the car and smiled at her. "We're here."

The parking lot was empty, except for their car, and she realized he wasn't kidding about the privacy. Her spirits rose. Maybe he intended to do more than just eat after all.

He handed her the blanket and took the basket himself. It was all so familiar that she had a moment of vertigo. Did their first picnic happen only a few days ago? Everything had changed so much since then. Changed in ways that she never could have predicted. She certainly never thought she'd see Geoffrey looking so happy, so easy-going, and so fucking hot.

He was killing her.

Sunny followed him into the greenhouse, almost heady from the aroma of flowers—especially roses—as they walked through the door. There wasn't a sound, except for their footsteps, and she expected the air to be humid and heavy, but it was surprisingly refreshing.

"This is really nice," she murmured.

"I've always liked it here."

"Do you come here often?" She was really asking if he ever brought another girl here.

"I've been known to spend a few quiet weekends here."

"Alone?" she blurted.

Geoffrey was apparently incapable of being flustered. "Have you ever seen me with another woman?"

"Well, it's not like I stalk you, Geoffrey. I mean, you have your private life."

"I've never brought anybody else here," he assured her.

"Not that it matters if you have," Sunny told him.

"Of course not."

"I was just a little curious."

"I understand." He led her to a wide stone bench and gestured at it. "Why don't you spread the blanket out there?"

Sunny did so and settled on the blanket, crossing one knee over the other. She watched silently as Geoffrey began unpacking the food, smiling widely as he pulled out a bottle of champagne. "You don't need to get me drunk, you know."

"I didn't intend to get you *drunk*," Geoffrey protested. "Would you like a glass?"

"Of course."

Geoffrey opened the champagne and poured them each a flute. Sunny accepted it greedily, happy to moisten her suddenly parched lips and tongue. As he moved, his shirt was pulled tight against his arms and chest, and she could see his muscles tense. He rarely wore clothes that showed off what a good body he had. She knew that he didn't think it was anything to brag about, probably because he wasn't as solid as Nash. But his lean body was still worth a second, third, and fourth look.

"Are you okay?" Geoffrey asked, as she held out her glass for a refill.

"Of course, why wouldn't I be?"

"You downed that champagne pretty fast," he observed.

"I was just a little thirsty."

"Just a little," Geoffrey murmured, watching the champagne pop and bubble in her flute. "Take this one a bit slower."

"I will," she promised, sipping from her glass to demonstrate.

Geoffrey finished unpacking the basket, laying before her a feast of delicacies, but Sunny wasn't interested. "You said the closet isn't how you wanted it for the first time."

"No. No, it wasn't."

"Is this what you had in mind for the first time? A picnic and a greenhouse and champagne?"

"No."

"Then what did you have in mind?"

"It was more like a dinner, candles, and wine. I had imagined taking you out and...wooing you," Geoffrey admitted. "I always had this romantic vision in mind."

"So why aren't we doing that?" Sunny asked. "I mean, not that I'd prefer it, but..."

"Because then I would have had to wait until tonight."

"Now who's impatient?" Sunny teased.

"Hey, I'm not impatient," Geoff protested. "I'm insatiable."

"There's a difference?"

"I think so. I want you all to myself this morning, and then tonight..."

Sunny's stomach dropped at the mention of the night, of future possibilities. She was ready to spend the night with Geoffrey and Nash. More than ready. Geoffrey might just be insatiable, but she felt insatiable and impatient.

"And then tonight?" she prompted.

"What do you want?"

"What do I want?"

"Yeah. Don't tell me you haven't been thinking about it."

"Oh, I'd never tell you that," Sunny said quickly. "I've been thinking about it a great deal."

"Here, try this."

Sunny accepted the small morsel of what might have been cheese. She wrinkled her nose and studied it. It didn't look like anything she had ever tried before, and she didn't know if she wanted to try it now. "What is it?"

"It's cheese."

"That's what I thought..." But she didn't bring it to her mouth.

"Try it," Geoffrey urged.

With a shrug, she put the entire piece in her mouth and chewed it slowly. The initial taste was surprising and unfamiliar, and her first reaction was to spit it out. But that didn't seem to be a good way to impress Geoffrey, so she continued to chew. And as she did, she began to realize that it didn't taste bad. It didn't taste bad at all. By the time she swallowed it, she wanted more.

Geoffrey smiled at the passing reaction on her face. "See, you can trust my taste."

"Well, your taste in lovers is impeccable," Sunny agreed. "I'm not really that hungry...for food."

"Oh?" He leaned forward, and she could tell that if she wanted, she could have him now. Perhaps he was tired of his own games.

"I think I'd like to take a walk."

He blinked, obviously surprised. She laughed with delight at his reaction. "A walk?"

"Yeah. I mean, it's a beautiful greenhouse. I want to see the roses. Perhaps you could show them to me?"

Geoffrey recovered quickly and stood, bending to take her hand. "I'd be delighted to show you the roses."

As soon as he touched her, Sunny realized she'd made a mistake. She wanted to feel his hands everywhere on her body, wanted to let him hold her, caress her, discover each inch of her. When he pulled her to her feet, she wanted him to yank her against him. She wanted to press her body against his, feel his heart beat against his chest, feel his warm breath on her face. She had been teasing him, but he would treat her request as something serious, and she was the one who'd suffer.

Geoffrey was surprisingly knowledgeable about roses. He rattled off little known facts and histories and even numbers, and Sunny tried to listen. She really did. She tried to pay attention to every word he said. But she loved the way he looked when he was explaining something. She loved the way his voice sounded when he was passionate about a topic. She had no idea what to make of the fact that roses were clearly a passion, but it hardly mattered. Everybody had to have a hobby after all.

"So what do you think?"

Sunny blinked and looked at the rose he was pointing at. "It's...beautiful."

Geoffrey smiled. "You didn't hear a word I said, did you?"

"No," Sunny admitted, averting her eyes.

"Where were you?"

"I was thinking about you."

"Oh? What about me?"

"How much I want to do this," Sunny answered, before launching herself into Geoffrey's arms. She kissed him like she had been dying to kiss him the day before. She'd spent the night fantasizing about him, fantasizing about his mouth, his lips, his lean body. He seemed surprised for a few seconds, but soon his arms were wrapped around her, and his tongue was sliding between her lips.

The kiss was different than anything they'd shared the day before. It was somehow more desperate and more hungry, yet less rushed. She wanted to kiss him thoroughly, wanted to explore his mouth completely, because she had the chance, because there was no hurry, because he was tied to her now, and she wanted to know every inch of him. Know the pressure of his mouth, the firmness of his lips.

Sunny was so caught up in the kiss that she didn't notice the water at first. The cold drops rolling down her neck could have been sweat. But she could only ignore it for a few seconds. Soon an entire torrent was released over their heads.

Sunny sprang away from Geoffrey, shocked and shivering. Her shirt was plastered to her skin, her hair already heavy against her face. Geoffrey looked just as surprised as she did, but, she thought, probably less like a drowned rat. "What is this?" she asked.

Geoffrey pointed up. "Sprinklers."

"Sprinklers?" Sunny squeaked. "Were these supposed to come on?"

Geoffrey shook his head. "There must be something wrong with the system."

Cold water poured down her face and back, and her skin erupted in goose bumps. She didn't have any desire to stand there for another second, and she sprinted toward their now soggy picnic. She heard Geoffrey following behind her, and now all she wanted to do was get out of the cold water and into the bright sunshine.

"Sunny...wait..." Geoffrey said, once she reached the bench.

"What?"

His fingers curled around her elbow and he spun her around. She caught herself against his chest and looked up into his dark eyes, mesmerized by the blue depths. Sunny caught her breath, staring at him questioningly. Water rolled down his face, drops hanging off his long eyelashes and getting caught on his lips. His shirt was cold and wet, but she could still feel the heat from his skin.

"God, Sunny," Geoffrey whispered.

Sunny forgot everything as soon as he spoke. The greenhouse could have flooded, and she wouldn't have noticed. The water on his lips tasted sweet as he pressed his mouth against hers once again. The system may have malfunctioned, but the timer in the sprinklers still worked, and the water stopped as suddenly as it began. Sunny didn't notice this time. She was too busy melting against Geoffrey.

Fire spread through her body, heating her blood, making her skin tingle. She clung to him, holding him as closely as she could, telling him with every movement of her lips, every soft moan, that she didn't want to let him go. And he seemed to feel the same way, seemed to be as hungry as she was. Sunny didn't mind completely losing track of the world, of everything that wasn't Geoffrey, as long as he was as lost as she was.

Geoffrey pushed her back until she was standing against the bench. She knew the blanket would be wet and the stone bench uncomfortable, but she didn't care. The memory of the day before only fed her hunger. She probably could have brought herself under control if she didn't know how Geoffrey felt when he was inside of her, if she didn't know how he sounded, if she didn't know how hot and strong he was, how good he felt.

They broke apart, gasping for air, but only an inch separated their mouths, like some magnetic force kept them from moving apart any further. "I need you now," she murmured, pawing at his wet jeans. They were stiff and didn't respond well to her attempts, but she kept trying.

Geoffrey caught her hands. "Sunny...Sunny...we can't here."

"Why not? We're alone."

"I know..."

"Geoffrey, please." She wasn't above pleading her case, even begging. It wasn't fair that he got to have hot sex with Nash all night, and she was left to suffer. She kissed him again, smashing her mouth against his. Before he could take the lead, she pulled away. "Please," she gasped.

Geoffrey whimpered, like she was the one holding out on him. "Come here," he said, pulling her toward the bench.

He surprised her by sitting down and pulling her onto his lap. Before she could ask him what he was doing, he had his hand up her skirt, his knuckles scraping against her inner-thigh. She spread her legs, allowing him access, pushing against his hand, silently encouraging him to continue. Her clit was already throbbing, and she squirmed on his lap, desperate to relieve the pressure building between her legs.

Geoffrey's large fingers pushed her thong aside and slid between her wet lips. She gasped his name as he finally found her clit, applying pressure on her delicate flesh with the pad of his finger. She panted and moaned as he began to rub her, but it still wasn't enough.

"More, Geoffrey. God, I need more."

Geoffrey obliged by shifting his hand, burying two fingers deep inside her while he massaged her clit with his thumb. She bucked against his hand, keening with pleasure as he found her G-spot with each thrust.

"I want to take you back to Nash's tonight," Geoffrey said, just loud enough for her to hear him over her rapid breathing. "I want to take you back to Nash's and stretch you out in his bed. I want to see what you look like against his silk sheets. I want to smell your perfume and his aftershave, and I want to taste your skin. I want to taste your skin when it's still slick with his sweat."

Sunny gasped. She could clearly see the picture he was painting. But it was his tone that made her quiver around his fingers more than his words. The last time he had talked to her like this, he sounded angry and desperate and confused. And now he was just being honest, telling her not only what she wanted, but what he expected to have.

"I've been wondering, Sunny, what it would feel like to fuck you while Nash fucks me. To have your soft body pressed against me, moving against mine, while Nash pounds into me. I have to admit, I probably wouldn't last as long as I'd like in that situation. You both feel too amazing separately, I can't even imagine what it would be like to feel the two of you at once. But that's okay. Do you know why?"

Sunny shook her head frantically. She didn't know why. At that moment, she didn't know a lot of things. If he kept talking like that, she wouldn't even know her own name.

"Has Nash ever fucked you in the ass?"

Sunny gasped. She couldn't even imagine Geoffrey saying *those* words to her, but he was. He was saying them, and he meant them, and his fingers were still thrusting into her. She shook her head. "No...no..."

"Would you like that? I want to fuck you while he takes you from behind, Sunny. Would you let me do that?"

"Yes. Yes." *Whatever you want.*

"Are you sure?"

"*Yes.*"

"Good," Geoffrey murmured. "Good."

"Good," Sunny echoed, wave after wave of pleasure rolling through her. "Oh...God..."

"I want to take you and Nash away for the weekend...or a week...and show you all the things I've thought about...dreamt about. I want to know every inch of you, Sunny. I want to taste you and feel you come against my mouth. I want to hear you scream until you're hoarse. I want to love you. Will you let me?"

"Yes," Sunny breathed. "Yes. Yes...oh...fuck..." She shook against his hand, her clit jerking and throbbing as the orgasm finally overtook her. She closed her eyes, throwing her head back, and riding out the waves of pleasure until she was exhausted. She collapsed against Geoffrey, resting her head on his shoulder.

Geoffrey brushed his lips across her cheek, and she sighed.

"That should hold me over for a little while," she murmured.

He chuckled softly and pulled his hand away, straightening her skirt.

"Did you mean it?"

"Yes. Which part?"

"About going away for the weekend?"

"Do you want to?"

"Where would we go?"

"We could get a flight up to San Francisco."

Sunny sat up, her eyes wide. "Really?"

"Why not?"

"Let's go to San Francisco, and get a big suite, and let's stay there for longer than a weekend."

Geoffrey frowned. "You know, this isn't going to work if you two never want to go back to work."

Sunny instantly deflated, worried that she had upset him. She opened her mouth to apologize, but he smiled and shook his head.

"I'm teasing you, Sunny. I'm sure your boss will understand."

Sunny beamed. "Let's go get ready. I need some time to pack and everything. Plus, Nash is probably still asleep."

Geoffrey released her, allowing her to stand. "You're awfully excited about this vacation. Somebody might think you haven't had one in years."

Sunny rolled her eyes. "Somebody would be right."

"Sorry, we just..."

"Need me to survive on a day to day basis?" Sunny smiled and kissed the corner of his mouth. "I know."

"We didn't eat any of my food," Geoffrey said, almost sadly.

"If you had asked, I could have told you that there was only thing I'm interested in," Sunny said, repacking the basket. "I mean, I like you for your mind, too. But, Geoffrey, I've been..."

"Waiting a long time, I know." He stood and picked up the damp blanket. "Sunny?"

"Hmm?"

"Did *you* mean it?"

"Yes. Which part?"

"That you love me."

Sunny smiled. "Yeah."

Geoffrey nodded. "Let's go fetch Nash, yeah?"

Sunny's smile widened. "He's going to be so surprised."

Geoffrey smirked. "To say the least."

CHAPTER 12

Nash tried to help plan their impromptu trip, but Geoffrey told him to pack and leave it all to him. It wasn't difficult to get three seats on a flight from LAX to San Francisco, and anybody with the money to spare would always be able to find a room in the Bay Area, regardless of how short the notice. Geoffrey was happy to deal with it all while he imagined Nash and Sunny packing, getting ready for the trip.

So much of the fears and concerns he harbored before were gone now. Nash hadn't told him that he loved him, but that didn't matter. They still had a strong connection. A connection that wouldn't be broken any time soon, or ever. And Sunny...

Well, he had never imagined anything so sweet.

Geoffrey couldn't tell them this. But he could show them. He could show them that he had a private commitment to them. Prove that he wasn't going to panic again and push them away.

Even if a part of him would always be a little worried that they would push him away. But Geoffrey understood there was always the chance for rejection, for pain, in any relationship. He could spend the rest of his life hiding from that—and, honestly, that had been his unstated plan—or he could take a chance, make a gamble, and come up a big winner.

The short flight up to San Francisco mostly passed in silence, but that was out of necessity. There was too much to be said, too many undercurrents of tension flowing between them. He could tell Sunny was still on edge, and he knew Nash well enough to know he was under a great strain. Geoffrey's nerves weren't doing too great either. They all had to pretend they were just normal people, going on a normal trip, or Geoffrey feared they would snap. And that was not socially acceptable behavior.

Sunny wanted the window seat, and Nash refused to sit in the middle, so Geoffrey gamely took the center seat. Wedged between both of them, all he could think about was the fantasy he had described to Sunny. There was something so alluring, so simply enthralling about the idea of being caught between somebody so soft, and somebody so hard. The thought held a nameless enchantment, like that was where he belonged, the space he was born to occupy.

His hand rested on Sunny's throughout the flight. His knee brushed against Nash's thigh. All he could think about was what would happen once they reached the hotel. Would they try to pretend they weren't there for one specific purpose? Would Sunny want to get dinner on the Pier? Would Nash insist on checking out the Bay? Would he think of a way to put off the inevitable?

Geoffrey didn't know what to do in such a situation.

Maybe push Sunny against the wall and tear her clothes off.

That plan definitely had its attraction.

"Are you nervous?" Nash murmured for Geoffrey's ears only.

Geoffrey offered a half shrug. "Are you?"

"What's there to be nervous about?"

"You tell me."

The corner of Nash's mouth lifted in a wry grin. "I've never had a threesome before."

"Really?"

"Why does that surprise you?" Nash asked, keeping his voice low.

"It seems like something you would try."

"Well, I came close once," Nash admitted.

"What happened?"

"The other guy chickened out. Didn't want to share his girlfriend after all. Also, I think he was afraid it would make him gay."

"Probably a common fear," Geoff murmured.

"What are you two whispering about over there?" Sunny asked, turning away from the window to look at them.

Geoffrey shook his head. "Nothing. Just Nash's sordid past."

She perked up, interested. "Oh?"

"I don't have a sordid past," Nash cut in.

"Pull the other one," Geoffrey mumbled. Sunny snickered.

"What was that?"

Geoffrey looked at him and said slowly and clearly, "Pull the other one. It has bells on it."

"Nice, Geoff."

"But you don't deny it."

"He won't tell me anything," Sunny said. "I've asked, but he always clams up. Makes me wonder what he's trying to hide."

"Oh, I can tell you what he's trying to hide."

Nash frowned and crossed his arms. "Don't think you're the only one with stories to tell."

"I'm shaking, Nash. Truly."

And with that, the tension that had been draped over them since they arrived at the airport dissipated. They spent the remaining twenty minutes of the flight laughing and swapping stories, Nash's face alternately going pale and turning purple, depending on the event Geoffrey chose to recount.

By the time they landed, Geoffrey was feeling a little high from their company and Sunny's eyes were gleaming. They were all in good spirits, and the spirits were sustained as they stepped out of the terminal into the cool San Francisco air. The sun was low in the sky and shrouded by clouds, but that didn't dampen their moods. If anything, it made Geoffrey more eager to get to their room.

The hotel wasn't far from the airport, and once again, Geoffrey was wedged between Nash and Sunny in the backseat. He knew he must have sat between them before. In the years they'd been working together, he must have been seated between the two of them at one point or another. But he couldn't remember ever being this tied up in knots. Every second, every block, brought them closer to the one thing he longed for. It was a curious mix of anticipation and nerves and excitement and fear and relief.

Sunny continued to hold his hand. Nash's leg was still against his.

They each only brought a single bag, so once they checked in, they didn't bother with a bellhop. Geoffrey appreciated the innate professionalism of the clerk when she handed them each a key to their single-bed suite.

The elevator ride to the appropriate floor was endless. Geoffrey tried to think of the last time he had done something like this. The fact was, he had never done anything like this. He had brought men and women home after a date with the intention of having sex, but not often. And occasionally he went home with somebody. But he had never gone to a neutral location, never brought his lovers to a hotel room, never experienced this level of adrenalin-pumping keenness.

The elevator dinged, startling him. The doors whooshed open. Nash stepped forward first, leading the way down the long corridor to their room. He couldn't help but wonder if Nash had done the same thing before—that seemed a given. Nash's exploits had never bothered Geoffrey before, even when he thought he could never have Nash. But now he was jealous. Not of the women, and men, who'd known him before, but of the experience.

He was beginning to understand about missed opportunities. Having nearly missed this one, all the others were coming back in a flood of regret.

Nash stepped aside to allow Geoffrey to unlock the door. It was only then that Geoffrey realized the key was still clutched in his clammy palm. Swallowing hard, he inserted the magnetic card into the lock and the light blinked green.

They filed into the room, and Geoffrey hung back, watching with amusement as Sunny made a beeline for the bathroom, and Nash headed directly to the closet. He took out each folded piece of laundry, carefully unfolded it, smoothed the wrinkles, and hung them in an orderly row. It was a routine that Nash went through in every hotel room, in every city.

Nash finished his ritual just as Sunny stepped out of the bathroom. They stood in the suite, facing each other in a slightly misshapen triangle. Geoffrey looked back and forth from Nash to Sunny, and none of them moved, as if they were all waiting for something. Geoffrey understood what he was waiting for—Nash to take the lead. Nash always took the lead. That was just the natural order of things.

Nash clearly did not intend to take the lead.

And Sunny was waiting on them. Which meant, she was waiting on him. He supposed that was fair enough. While the situation wasn't his idea, the location was. The neutral territory. The whisking away to the Bay Area for an impromptu holiday. The declaration, if not in words, that they were together, a unit.

Geoffrey took the first step, walking into the middle of the room. Now instead of a triangle, they formed a crooked line. As he suspected, that was all that was necessary. As soon as he moved, both Nash and Sunny took a step toward him. And he was within inches of his goal, within inches of being completely surrounded.

Geoffrey reached out with both hands, snagging Sunny's shirt and

Nash's belt. He pulled them close to him, and they touched him at the same time. Sunny's smaller hands were on his shoulders, Nash's on his hips, and Geoffrey realized the hard part was over. He tilted his head and Nash kissed him softly, as though he was seeking some sort of invitation. Sunny's lips were hot on his neck, teasing the skin just below his hairline. Geoffrey shivered, opening his mouth to Nash's kiss.

He could feel Sunny step away, and he tried to pull away from Nash to see what she was doing, but Nash didn't release him. She was back in seconds though, and she gathered up his shirt, exposing his abdomen and ribs, then pressed her chest against his bare back.

"I told Nash," Sunny said, her lips moving against his skin as she spoke. "What you told me."

Geoffrey broke the kiss and looked at Nash. "Oh, really?"

Sunny nodded. "Yes, we talked on the phone."

"And what did Nash say to that?"

"He said he liked your ideas quite a bit," Sunny said, sliding her hands over his ribs. "So much so, he couldn't decide which one he liked more."

"I like them both quite a bit myself," Geoffrey admitted. "I don't know which one I like more. Would you like to choose?"

Sunny's hand moved down his stomach and rested on the button of his jeans. Nash was looking at him with dark, amused eyes, like he had a joke he didn't want to share. "Sunny has a hard time making up her mind, too."

"I see," Geoffrey breathed as her hands moved over his growing erection.

"So you might have to tell us," Nash continued.

"If she keeps that up, I won't be able to tell you anything," Geoffrey protested, as Sunny worked his zipper down and slipped her fingers into his pants. Her fingertips caressed his shaft with hardly any pressure.

"Sunny, stop that. It's not very nice. Do you know what you want?"

Geoffrey couldn't see her face, but he could hear her smile. "I want him to fuck me, Nash."

Nash's eyes were positively dancing. "Then I guess we know how we're going to start."

"I guess so," Geoffrey breathed.

He grabbed Sunny's wrists and pried her hands away from his crotch. He pulled her around to face him, and before she could speak, backed her up to the bed. She looked up at him with wide eyes and sat down heavily on the mattress. She put her foot on his thigh, smiling at him coquettishly.

"Can you help me finish undressing?"

Geoffrey looked over his shoulder to Nash. "If you'll look in my bag, you'll see I brought certain…supplies."

Nash grinned. "You're such a Boy Scout."

"Yeah, I'm pretty sure what I'm about to do is not in the manual," Geoffrey murmured as he pulled Sunny's T-shirt over her head. She wasn't wearing a bra, and her nipples were already hard, a deep pink, and looking delicious.

"If not, it should be," Sunny said, dropping back on her elbows. Her dark hair fell in waves around her face and shoulders, a sharp contrast to her pale skin.

Geoffrey snorted. "Well, I probably could have used the pointers."

"If yesterday and this morning are anything to go by, you don't need pointers," Sunny said.

"I second that," Nash said, coming up behind him with a handful of condoms and a large bottle of lubricant. "Jeez, Geoff, you have enough stuff here for a couple of weeks."

"I plan to stay busy," Geoffrey replied without looking over his shoulder. His attention was focused on the buttons of Sunny's pants. He slipped them out one at a time, slowly exposing Sunny's skin to his touch. She lifted her hips, silently encouraging him to drag the pants down her thighs.

"I'd say. I don't know, I'm starting to think Geoffrey isn't quite the innocent we all assumed he was," Nash said, tossing the condoms on the bed.

Sunny smirked. "Maybe he's more of a gentleman than an innocent."

Geoffrey tossed the pants aside and stepped back, momentarily content to simply study Sunny's naked body. He had touched her, kissed her, fucked her, but he never had the chance to simply look at her. Her shoulders were sloped back, pushing her perfect breasts forward. They were just big enough to fill his palms, and her nipples were begging to be licked, sucked, and nibbled. Her stomach was flat but defined, a clear sign of her regular work-out schedule. Her thighs were white and strong, her legs long, her calves exquisitely shaped. He could still feel those perfect legs wrapped around him as he thrust into her, and the memory of that alone was enough to make him hard.

The hair between her legs was a few shades darker than the hair on her head, and the curls were already damp with her arousal. He didn't move to touch her, but he could tell by the quickening of her breath that his slow perusal had the same affect as a caress. He could feel Nash beside him, not quite touching him, and knew Nash was gaping at her as well. Sunny didn't seem to mind the attention.

"She's perfect, isn't she?" Nash asked.

Geoffrey could merely nod.

"I'm cold and lonely, too," Sunny said, holding out her hand. "Why don't one of you join me instead of gawking at me?"

Geoffrey finished undressing quickly, feeling that no further invitation was necessary. But Nash didn't move to join them. He stood at the foot of the bed, his arms crossed over his naked chest.

"Nash?" Geoffrey asked.

"I just want to look at you both." Nash narrowed his eyes slightly. "Kiss her."

"You're the boss, boss," Sunny said, draping her arm over Geoffrey's shoulder and pulling him closer.

Geoffrey felt self-conscious as he returned Sunny's kiss. He could feel Nash's gaze on him, feel the weight of his stare. He kept his own eyes closed, so he wouldn't have to look at the other man. But within seconds, he forgot that Nash was there, studying them, and focused entirely on Sunny. Her lips were hot and demanding, and she pushed him flat on the bed, swinging one leg over his hips to straddle him. She rocked her hips, sliding her pussy along his shaft, coating him in her juices, teasing him.

Geoffrey moaned, wrapping his hands around her waist to hold her still. It was like holding dynamite. He could feel the energy in her tense, trembling muscles. He knew that if he let her go, she would unleash herself on him, finally taking what she wanted, what she was pleading for earlier that day. Geoffrey could only think of one reason to stop her, and he opened his eyes, seeking out Nash over her shoulder.

Nash was completely undressed now, and the sight of him was a blow to the solar plexus. He was standing at the foot of the bed, his arms crossed, his dark eyes heavy, and he was just perfect. Geoffrey drew Nash's attention to Sunny with his eyes, and Nash nodded, understanding Geoffrey's silent question.

Sunny shifted forward again, sliding his cock between her lips. They both moaned from the contact, and something flickered in Nash's eyes.

Geoffrey flipped her over onto her back quickly, kneeling between her legs. She wrapped her legs around him instantly, lifting her hips. He couldn't quite believe that she was so ready, so impatient for him. He couldn't believe it, but he certainly understood it. His cock was achingly hard, the tip already wet with pre-come, and his balls felt heavy. It was a rush to want somebody, something, so completely, and finally have it.

The bed dipped behind him as Nash kneeled on the edge. He ran his hand down Geoffrey's spine, pushing him forward slightly. Geoffrey obliged, adjusting himself so that both Sunny and Nash could be comfortable. Nash slid his fingers along the crack of Geoffrey's ass, not quite tickling him, but inducing a series of shudders. He reached between Geoffrey's legs and cupped his balls, rolling them between his fingers and tugging on them gently.

Geoffrey released his breath in a long sigh. Sunny grunted softly and pushed her hips forward again. Nash squeezed him a bit harder and chuckled. "Better give her what she wants."

Geoffrey didn't need to be told twice, but a part of his mind was still on Nash. He wished he could see what the other man was doing, but he couldn't look over his shoulder. It was impossible to direct his attention away from Sunny and her soft, flushed, gleaming body. He thrust into her slowly, gripping his self-control tightly. He didn't want to lose it yet. He didn't have the chance to really enjoy her before, to really get to know her body, and he wasn't about to rush this.

Sunny shifted, meeting him thrust for thrust, her hands clenching the bed. Her knuckles were white, her head tilted back, her creamy throat exposed. She wasn't shouting yet, but she was breathing hard, and her moans were growing in volume and strength.

Sunny's body was so hot, it burned him, warmed him completely. He was lost in that heat when Nash gently pushed one well-lubed finger into his ass. Geoffrey stiffened and yelped at the sudden cold contact, and Nash put a soothing hand on his shoulder.

"Relax," he murmured. "I didn't mean to startle you."

Geoffrey took a deep breath, his cock buried in Sunny. She was panting, looking at him like she didn't understand what was happening.

"It's okay," he breathed.

Nash began moving his finger slowly, sliding in and out, and then added a second finger, and things were more than okay.

Geoffrey was forced to move his hips slower, but he lifted Sunny's hips a little higher off the bed, angling himself for deeper strokes. Her eyes clouded over with the adjustment, and he thought that would keep her satisfied while Nash continued to prepare him, one deliberate motion at a time.

Geoffrey's pulse hammered, and he thought the anticipation couldn't be good for his blood pressure. His mind raced ahead several steps, trying to get ahead of his body, trying to imagine exactly the way Nash would feel behind him while Sunny clenched and quivered around his cock. Geoffrey was nearly begging by the time Nash inserted a third finger, the words were half-whimpers. His own fingers were shaking slightly, and he gripped Sunny tighter to hide the effect they were having on him.

Nash's hand disappeared, leaving Geoff feeling bereft. The mattress shifted again, and Geoffrey didn't have to look to know that Nash was kneeling behind him, his cock hard and slick. "Are you ready?" Nash breathed.

Geoffrey nodded, forcing himself to relax, even as he braced himself for the initial breach. It was easier than the first time, the sensation less shocking. Geoffrey held his breath as Nash slid into him, and even Sunny stopped moving. She clenched around him as Nash became fully seated, and Geoffrey gasped, moaned, and shouted all at once. The blood drained from his head, heat spread through his body, and the most exquisite combination of pleasure and pain clenched him, like a giant fist around his chest.

"Move forward," Nash encouraged.

Geoffrey blinked, wondering if he could ever move again. Nash gripped his hip and squeezed him gently, silently repeating his request. Geoffrey nodded, rocking his hips forward. Nash didn't move with him, instead pulling half-way out. Geoffrey leaned back, Nash moved forward, and Sunny pushed her hips up. It was like finding the right beat to dance to, making his body move to a rhythm he couldn't hear, but he could feel.

He forced himself to concentrate on the simple mechanics of the act until everything happened like second nature. If he thought about what he was doing, he'd falter, or miss a beat, but if he relaxed and turned himself over to the natural flow, then it seemed his body knew exactly what to do. Like he had been made for this, born to be in this position, with these two people.

Geoffrey didn't know how long he could maintain his composure. He felt like he was going to shatter. It was too much for any human body to withstand. It was too much to keep from flying apart. He couldn't stand to look away from Sunny, but he couldn't stand to look at her either. And through it all, Nash kept talking to him. Muttering little things in his ear, little words that he didn't always catch, but it didn't matter. His voice was low and silky, his breath warm on Geoffrey's damp skin.

"God, Geoffrey, you're so tight. Fuck. I love the way you feel. Oh, yes...do that again..."

Geoffrey didn't even know what he did. Nash was hitting his prostrate with each thrust, and lights were flashing before his eyes. Somehow he found the presence of mind to realize that he was getting close, and he needed Sunny to come first. He planned to make her come as much as possible, and he needed this first one. He released the tight grip he had on her hip and found her swollen clit.

"Oh, God, Geoff! Geoff, yes. More. Fuck. Fuck..."

Her words, barely coherent, pushed him that much closer to the edge. He clenched around Nash, his muscles tensed, his skin felt tight. Sunny arched back, shouting his name. The shout echoed above their heads as her pussy contracted and fluttered around his shaft. He tumbled after her, the orgasm building at the base of his spine and pushed through his body with one hard, direct thrust from Nash. His muscles convulsed, and the lights that had been flashing before his eyes flared and completely obscured his vision. The only thing that kept him from falling forward was Nash's arm, wrapped around him tightly, holding him back against his strong chest.

Distantly, he heard Nash's shout of release, and felt his cock jerk. That moment seemed to stretch, freeze in time, that scant second when he could feel the aftershocks of Sunny's orgasm echoing through his own body to meet the trembling of Nash's. Sunny stopped vibrating first, relaxing against the bed, and then Nash rested his forehead on Geoffrey's shoulder and released a long, shuddering sigh.

Geoffrey opened his mouth like he was going to speak, but his tongue was dry, his throat sore. Had he been shouting? He didn't remember shouting, but he knew if he spoke now, his words would be hoarse. Sunny smiled at him, looking content and sated and sleepy.

"I think that was worth the wait," Sunny murmured.

Nash nodded, his forehead still resting on Geoffrey's shoulder.

Sunny moved first, gently pulling away from him and rolling to her side, making room for him to collapse. Fortunately, Nash didn't just release him and let him fall flat on his face, and Geoffrey appreciated that. Without releasing him, Nash lowered them to the mattress,

Geoffrey tucked between his body and Sunny's. As soon as he was comfortable on the bed, he reached for her, pulling her close against him. Their sweat and breath mingled, and they were a tangle of exhausted limbs.

"When's round two?" Sunny asked.

"You're ready for round two?" Geoffrey asked incredulously, his lips moving against her salty skin.

"Aren't you?"

"No," Geoffrey and Nash said at the same time.

"What's the point of having two of you then?"

"Give us a minute, Sunny. I don't know about Geoffrey, but I don't have the same constitution I did at eighteen."

"So you're saying I need to find two eighteen-year-olds?"

"No," they both said again.

She smiled and burrowed closer, her ass fitting snuggly against Geoffrey's groin. "Well, I suppose you'll do."

"Don't worry," Nash said, "you're going to be begging us to stop."

"I don't believe it."

"You haven't seen what's in Geoffrey's bag of goodies over there."

Sunny looked over her shoulder. "What have you got?"

Geoffrey only smiled.

CHAPTER 13

Their room had an amazing view of the bay, but Sunny barely noticed. She barely noticed anything about the room except the bed, which was big enough to fit all three of them comfortably. She couldn't keep her eyes open. She resisted the urge to fall asleep as much as possible, but the fact was, she hadn't slept at all in the past three days, and Geoffrey felt amazing.

Sunny blinked, closing her eyes for just a moment, and when she opened them again, the shadows were in the wrong place. She frowned, glancing at the digital clock next to the bed. It had to be wrong. At least three hours off.

"I think she's awake," Geoffrey murmured.

Sunny smiled and stretched before turning over to face them. Geoffrey was on his back, and Nash had his legs draped over Geoffrey's thighs, his body almost covering Geoff's. His mouth was busy, covering Geoffrey's neck and chest in small kisses. Geoffrey sighed and arched his neck, running his hands down Nash's back lightly. Geoffrey's eyes were half-closed, but he didn't look tired. She wondered if he had napped as well.

"Was I asleep long?"

"Couple of hours," Geoffrey said, his lips barely moving. Nash glanced at her from beneath his long lashes, but he didn't stop exploring Geoffrey's skin with his mouth.

"Did you two keep each other occupied?"

"Mmmm," Nash answered against Geoffrey's shoulder.

119

Sunny pushed the sheet off of them, exposing Geoffrey's hard cock. The light in the room was dim, but bright enough for her to study his body closely. She hadn't yet had the chance to really see him, to take her time with him the way she liked, using her eyes, her hands, and her mouth. Nash looked up then and he must have noticed the hunger in her eyes, because he smiled at her.

"Why don't you have a taste?" Nash asked, his question low and knowing. He rolled away from Geoffrey, stretching out on his side.

Sunny didn't miss the way Geoffrey responded to Nash's question. It was subtle, but unmistakable. His body trembled and his cock jerked and his breath caught in his throat. She wondered how many times he had thought of her swallowing his cock, how many times he had imagined her wrapping her lips around his shaft, tonguing his head, teasing his balls. She loved to let her mind drift that direction. She loved to think of him thinking of her.

Sunny moved without answering, settling on the mattress between his legs and stretching out on her stomach. She gently pushed his legs apart, caressing his inner thighs until he sucked his breath in sharply and tensed. Some areas were more sensitive than others, and she carefully explored each broad thigh until she could pinpoint the exact location of each spot that would make him hiss and jerk.

She followed her fingers with her mouth, licking and sucking on those magic little spots until he was panting her name. His cock was long and hard, and practically begging her to lick the drops of clear fluid away from his slit. She looked up to see that they were both watching her, two pairs of dark, fascinated eyes. She knew exactly what Nash liked, knew exactly how to turn him into a big pile of goo with nothing more than a few well-placed, well-timed swipes of her tongue. But what did Geoffrey like? Her stomach tensed with anticipation and excitement at the thought. God, she wanted to know, couldn't wait to find out.

No doubt, Nash already knew what Geoffrey liked. She paused a moment, waiting for the cold hand of jealousy to grip her. She didn't know who she should be jealous of, or why, but she knew that it should be a standard, common reaction. But instead of a chill, she just felt very warm. Her lips curled into a slow smile.

"Nash…why don't you come down here and help me out?"

He arched his eyebrow. "I never thought you were the sort to need help."

"I want to make sure I do it right. You never get a second chance at a first impression, after all."

Nash's smile matched hers. "That's true."

Sunny winked at Geoffrey. "You okay there, slugger? You sound a little short of breath."

His mouth opened and closed and opened again. "I...I'm good."

Nash slid down the bed and propped his head on his hand. He watched her with lazy eyes and dragged one large finger down the underside of Geoffrey's shaft, coming to a rest at the base.

"Start here with your tongue," he murmured. "Then follow my finger." He traced his fingertip around Geoffrey's balls slowly. Geoffrey moaned softly.

Sunny nodded. "I think I can handle that."

She started where Nash indicated, at the base of Geoffrey's cock, then slowly dragged her tongue around his sac. His skin was loose and salty and smelled musky, smelled like sex. She felt, rather than heard, him moan, and she was suddenly curious about how much he could handle, how long she could make this last. She sucked one of his balls, then the other, between her lips, fluttering her tongue against his tender flesh.

"Oh, my God, *Sunny*."

Nash ran his hand down her back, skimming her skin. She shivered in response to his light touch, unconsciously spreading her legs, silently asking him to move lower.

"Anybody ever do that to you before, Geoff?" Nash asked.

"I...no. No...never."

Sunny would have smiled if her mouth was free.

"That's not all she can do," Nash murmured.

It was far from all she could do. Sunny gave good head, and she knew it. She liked to make sure her lovers knew it as well. It was probably one of her favorite things to do. She loved every part of it, loved the way the simple act assaulted her senses and set her nerves on fire. Sometimes she could get off without any physical contact—though she desperately wanted it now. She raised her hips off the bed, pushing her ass in the air, exposing her swollen pussy to Nash's fingers.

Geoffrey rested his palm on the back of her head lightly, his fingers threading through her hair. She didn't resist the contact, and he didn't increase the pressure. She continued to focus on his balls, ignoring his cock. She didn't touch him, her hands splayed across his thighs. She dragged her tongue across his skin and blew lightly on the damp skin, delighted by the way his thighs tensed.

Nash continued to tease her, caressing her thighs. His knuckles brushed against her lips, and her pussy clenched, sending spasms up her abdomen with each hint of contact. She couldn't believe how much she wanted them, how much she still needed the contact, the attention. It was like their previous encounter had never happened, and she knew if her mouth wasn't already busy, she'd be begging Nash to fuck her.

And Geoffrey sounded like *he* was nearly prepared to beg *her*. She finally moved one hand from his thigh, slipping it behind his scrotum to find the sensitive skin there. He jerked suddenly, his hips lifting off the bed as she teased him with the tip of her finger. He made a funny whimpering sound in the back of his throat, like he was keeping words trapped there. She'd find a way to free them.

Sunny pulled both his balls into her mouth at once, sucking gently and humming. Her clit was pulsing now, her juices flowing freely. She thought Nash would never stop teasing her, and she didn't understand why he was being so cruel. Geoffrey whimpered again, echoing her frustration, and Sunny realized what Nash was doing. There was only one way to end her own torment.

She moved her finger, slipping it past Geoff's tight ring of muscle and seeking out his prostate.

"Oh, Sunny, just…"

He never had a chance to finish what he was going to say. She ran her tongue up his shaft and wrapped her lips around his head. Her assumption had been correct. As soon as Geoffrey's torment ended, hers did as well. Nash lapped the juices from her flesh, circling her entry with the tip of his tongue, before plunging it deep inside her pussy.

Sunny clenched around his tongue and moaned around Geoffrey's cock. Nash gripped her hips and fucked her with his mouth, his lips hard, his tongue fast. It was a searing, stunning contrast to the way she used her mouth on Geoffrey. Each stroke was long, hot, and deliberate. Geoffrey tried to make her move faster, but she put one small hand on his thigh, pressing him back to the mattress.

As much as she wanted to devote all her energy and attention to Geoffrey, Nash's tongue was making her crazy, disrupting her concentration. She wanted to feel Nash's cock slam into her, but she knew that would distract her utterly from Geoffrey. Instead of asking for more, she relaxed her jaw and swallowed Geoffrey's cock, her throat muscles flexing around the tip of his cock.

Nash found her clit, pinching it gently. She bucked against his hand, her head spinning. The pressure of Geoffrey's cock in her throat, the hungry sounds he made, the taste of his salty skin, the slickness of his pre-come against the back of her tongue, made her heart pound an erratic rhythm, and Nash's tongue seemed to reach every inch of her...

And suddenly, Nash's tongue was gone. She groaned in disappointment. She glanced up and noticed Geoffrey's gaze wasn't on her. He seemed to be looking over her head. She felt the bed shift, and realized Nash didn't plan to leave her. He slammed his cock into her exactly the way she wanted. The contact was so sudden, so welcome, so *needed*, that she almost came with the first thrust.

"Sunny...faster...please. Just a little bit faster," Geoffrey moaned.

She might not have paid any attention to his plea, but she needed to come. She didn't have the self-control to resist it, and she didn't have the strength to fight against the hard, fast pace Nash was setting. Sunny began moving her head quickly, moving his hand from his thigh and allowing him to thrust his hips to meet her on each stroke.

"Oh...Sunny. Fuck. *Yes*."

Geoffrey shot his load deep in her throat, coming in several quick spasms. As soon as he erupted in her throat, she reached her climax, her pussy clenching and shuddering around Nash's cock repeatedly. She pulled her hand away from Geoffrey, letting his cock slip from her mouth, but Nash didn't stop. Each time he slammed into her pussy, she convulsed again, tiny tremors like electric bursts making her muscles clench.

"Nash...oh fuck...Nash...you're killing me...oh fuck...I can't...I can't take this..."

"Just a little bit more..."

"Nash...please...*please*..." She knew he was going to kill her. He was going to tear her apart. She didn't know if she was going to come again, or if she ever stopped coming. That question was answered when she met Geoffrey's eyes again, and saw desire and satisfaction and pleasure lurking in their blue depths. Sunny realized that he liked to watch them, and it was his heated expression that sent her spiraling into her second orgasm.

Sunny shouted something incoherent, the effort ripping her throat. Nash cursed under his breath and stiffened behind her, thrusting into her one final time before following her over the edge.

She collapsed on Geoffrey, and Nash fell beside them, and all three of them were panting.

"Oh, my God," Geoffrey murmured.

Sunny smiled at him lazily. "I don't feel like you've seen my best work. Nash was keeping me off my game."

Nash merely snorted.

"You were distracting me," Sunny said defensively.

"You better get used to it," Nash countered. "I have a feeling that none of us is interested in playing fair."

"I am," Geoffrey said, though it seemed to take a great deal of effort. Sunny smirked with satisfaction. He would be incoherent and fuzzy for the next several minutes at least.

"No, you're not," Sunny assured him. "Then it wouldn't be as much fun."

"Seriously, Sunny, that was…"

"Amazing? I know."

Nash grinned, running his hand over Geoffrey's tight stomach. "Beautiful, talented, *and* modest. That's a killer combination."

"Indeed," Geoffrey agreed, propping himself up on his elbows. "I'm hungry."

"What do you want to do about it?" Sunny asked.

"Get some food."

"There's a restaurant in the lobby," Nash volunteered.

"I don't think it's a good idea to be seen in public with the two of you," Sunny countered. At their baffled looks, she grinned and added, "I can't keep my hands to myself."

"Room service, then?" Geoffrey asked.

"Room service," she confirmed.

CHAPTER 14

Nash didn't think he was hungry until the food Geoffrey ordered arrived, and then he was ravenous. He could see the amusement on Sunny's face as he dug into the food, like he hadn't eaten in at least a week. He just smiled back and started work on the stack of waffles— Geoffrey had chosen several items off of each menu, giving them a wide array of breakfast, lunch, and dinner foods.

"Are you going to save any for the rest of us?" Sunny asked.

"There's plenty here. Besides, I need to keep my strength up," Nash answered around a mouthful of eggs.

"I don't think you'll have any problem with that."

Geoffrey was quiet, eating without comment. Nash recognized that sort of silence. He had seen Geoffrey retreat into himself like that when he was tired, or trying to work out a new, never before seen, problem. A slight frown creased his brow, and his eyes were thoughtful. Nash realized he could probably devote an entire day to watching Geoff and cataloguing each expression and quirk of his lips.

Geoffrey was sitting at the table, while he and Sunny were sharing the bed. Geoff wore a robe that barely covered his chest and legs. His hair was a tussled mess, and he had marks all over his neck and shoulders. Some were larger than others and could have only been made by Nash, though he did see the evidence of hickeys from Sunny's smaller mouth.

He might have felt Nash's gaze on him, because he looked up quickly and their eyes caught. Nash smiled and Geoffrey lifted the corners of his mouth in return. His cheeks were already dark with stubble, which Nash found far too distracting. Geoffrey's five o'clock shadow had never distracted him before, but now he couldn't look away from it.

"Hey, Earth to Nash…"

"What?"

Sunny pointed to his plate. "You're about to spill scrambled eggs all over your lap."

"Oh. Thanks."

"It's why I'm here."

Nash returned her smile, and realized he was never going to get any work done at all. How could he be expected to worry about numbers and clients and the boring minutiae of running a business when Sunny and Geoffrey were in touching distance? Every time he left his office, or looked out the door, or spoke to one of them on the phone, or even over e-mail, he'd be tempted to abandon his real work. He knew that this was a bad thing, but he didn't really care too much. It was his firm, after all, and if he wanted to spend office hours fucking his partner and his assistant, then who was going to stop him?

Geoffrey probably would stop me, Nash thought ruefully. He liked being the responsible one, and he'd put the success of the business over his own personal pleasure.

Which was why it was so good to have Geoffrey around, but Nash was still going to do his best to thwart those tendencies.

"Can we do some sightseeing tomorrow?" Sunny asked.

"If you can walk tomorrow," Geoffrey said casually.

Nash snorted. He loved the way Geoffrey could still surprise him. He'd just never expected to hear those kind of words leaving Geoffrey's mouth, but Nash was quickly coming to realize that Geoffrey had an entire side—a teasing, sensual side—that he never let the world see. He never really thought of Geoffrey as a sexual creature, but the other man was full of surprises.

Sunny chuckled and stretched her legs. "I don't think I quite need bed rest yet."

"The night's young." Nash finished his eggs and set his plate aside, then reached for a sandwich. "But I have always wanted to see Alcatraz."

"You've seen Alcatraz," Geoffrey said.

"No, I haven't."

"Yes, you have."

"When?"

"When we came up here for spring break. I'm not surprised you don't remember, but we were definitely there. And I have the pictures to prove it."

Nash frowned. "Spring break? I don't remember that at all."

"You were pretty wasted."

"For the entire weekend?"

"Yes."

Nash grimaced. "Well, maybe I'll remember it this time."

Geoffrey sipped from a glass of orange juice. "Probably."

Geoffrey's voice was still hoarse from the all the screaming and moaning. Nash liked the way he sounded.

As they each finished eating, they gradually cleared off the bed, moving the stack of dishes back to the rolling tray. Nash had to make sure all the plates were stacked the right way, all the crumbs were wiped away, and everything was back in its place. He glanced over to Geoff and Sunny while he worked, but neither of them seemed the least impatient or put-out with his dallying. They sat side by side on the bed, both partially naked, both waiting for him, both looking at him with bright eyes.

Nash discarded his robe and crawled onto the bed, wedging himself between them, his back against the headboard. As soon as he was settled, Sunny straddled his lap and allowed him to push her robe from her shoulders. Her long hair fell down her back and, as always, he was fascinated by the contrast between her creamy shoulders and her dark tresses. She dipped her head and kissed him slowly. He relaxed against the headboard and wrapped his arm around her, pulling her deeper into the kiss.

Sunny rocked against him, her damp pussy sliding against his growing erection. She broke from his lips, kissing along his jaw until she reached his ear. She spoke in a low voice, as though she was sharing some dark secret. "I want both of you to fuck me, Nash. I've wanted the two of you for so long."

Nash looked over her shoulder to meet Geoffrey's eyes. One glance assured him that Geoffrey had heard her, too. He stripped his robe away, and his cock was already hard. Nash nodded, directing Geoffrey with his eyes.

"I want that, too," Nash murmured, kissing her neck. He moved his mouth lower and pushed her back gently, his mouth seeking out her full breasts. He pulled her nipple between his teeth, rolling his tongue against her skin. Each time she squirmed against him, his cock jerked and his groin tightened. She was already wet for them.

He was well acquainted with the feel and smell of Sunny's skin, but now something was a little different about it—Geoffrey. Geoffrey's cologne and sweat and musk were all over her, changing the way she tasted. The realization made his stomach drop, made his mouth water. A dozen different scenarios instantly bombarded his mind's eye— going down on her after Geoffrey fucked her, licking his jizz from her skin, sucking the taste of Sunny's arousal from Geoffrey's cock.

"God, Nash," she moaned, running her fingers through his hair. He moved from one nipple to the other, his tongue swirling around the hardening flesh and creating patterns of pleasure. Each time she rocked against him, her desire was more obvious, and he knew he wouldn't get away with teasing her for much longer. Sunny always knew what she wanted and she wasn't shy about taking it.

Nash lifted his head and caught Geoffrey's eye again. They shared a small smile while Geoffrey squeezed a good amount of lube onto his fingers. While Nash was distracted by what Geoffrey was doing, Sunny reached between their bodies and found his cock, squeezing it lightly.

"Wait a second," he muttered, lifting her off his lap. She looked disappointed, until she saw he was merely repositioning himself. He pushed himself to his knees, then sat back on his heels and pulled her back.

Sunny wrapped her legs around his waist and lowered herself to his cock, sliding onto his shaft slowly. Nash wrapped his arms around her, holding her close while he looked for the right rhythm. She hissed and moaned, throwing her head back while he moved in short, slow strokes. She fluttered and tensed around him, tight and unbelievably hot. Every time he fucked her, it was almost like the first time. She just didn't *feel* like any woman he had been with before, and somehow, he always forgot just how amazing she was.

Sunny tensed suddenly, her walls clamping around his cock. He didn't have to look to know that Geoffrey had pushed his fingers in her ass, preparing to give her exactly what she asked for. Nash slowed his thrusts, wanting to work with Geoffrey. He was moving slowly, deliberately, so Nash moved at the same pace. Sunny's cheeks were flushed, her eyes bright, her bottom lip caught between her teeth.

"How does that feel?" he asked.

"Oh…fuck…"

"That mean it feels good?"

She nodded frantically, her fingers curling into his shoulders. "Just...slow. Please...go slowly..." The words came in short bursts. She was already panting, and she kept flexing around his cock, which meant he had a very hard time concentrating.

"I'll go slow," Geoffrey promised.

Sunny shivered, the tremors moving down her body and directly through Nash's cock. "Christ," he sighed.

Nash watched as Geoffrey pulled his hand from Sunny and slipped a condom over his shaft. He moved quickly, applying lube to his sheathed cock before positioning himself behind Sunny.

"Sunny," Nash said, gripping her hip and forcing her to stop. "You ever do anything like this before?"

She shook her head.

"We're going to have to stop for a second so Geoffrey can fuck you. Hold still and relax."

Geoffrey leaned forward to kiss her shoulder. "He's bossy, but he has a point. Try to relax."

"How can I relax?"

Geoffrey rested a hand on her shoulder and rubbed his fingers over her skin absently. She shivered again, prompting a sigh from Nash. He resisted the urge to close his eyes, though. He wanted to see Geoffrey slide into her, and he wanted to see the look on her face, wanted to witness every emotion and passing thought until she was simply incoherent. He also wanted to watch Geoff's face, wanted to see how the tightness and the heat affected him.

Nash consciously took slow, deep breaths, hoping Sunny would mimic him. He could feel it when Geoffrey first entered her, and then he could feel each glorious, maddening inch after that. He hadn't counted on how good Geoffrey's cock would feel as it slid into Sunny's ass and created a soft friction against his own shaft. Soon, they were both in Sunny completely, her thin skin the only thing that separated their cocks, though he could still feel the added heat from Geoffrey's skin.

"Oh, God," Sunny panted. "Oh God, oh God, oh God... God... Nash... Geoff.... fuck..."

The tendons in Geoffrey's neck were standing out, and his jaw was tight. Nash could tell he was using every bit of self-control he had to hold himself back, to keep from going as fast and hard as he wanted. Nash nodded at him, indicating he should move first.

Geoffrey pulled back, but not out of her completely, and then rocked forward again. Even though they hadn't been together for terribly long, Nash already understood how Geoffrey's body worked, and was able to follow his rhythm naturally. They rocked forward and back at the same time, not fighting for Sunny's body between them, but letting her get caught up, like a leaf caught in a river's current.

Nash didn't care how fast or slow they moved. All he cared about was the closeness, the proximity, the actual physical contact. Feeling them both at the same time, knowing that they couldn't get closer, looking up to watch them both, gripping Sunny's hip in one hand, and reaching out to Geoffrey with the other—this was what he wanted. Moving with both of them, falling into a rhythm with them, like it was the most natural thing in the world, feeling her hot breath on his face, and listening to Geoffrey's harsh gasps, knowing his heartbeat echoed theirs—it was intoxicating. Fascinating. Overwhelming.

And they were his.

Something red and sharp and hot and piercing shot through his body, stole his breath from him. His stomach, chest, and throat clenched, his cock jerked, his balls ached. He didn't know if either one of them could see the sudden change, but he wouldn't be surprised if they could. Wouldn't be surprised if it was written all over his face, glowing like a neon sign in his eyes. The feeling, the sensation, the emotion was so alien, and so familiar, and he didn't quite know its name, but he knew exactly what it was.

They were *his*. They belonged to him and *with* him. They wanted him, and they loved him, and he loved them, too.

"Oh, God," Nash gasped. "Oh, my God."

Sunny seemed to be too distracted to notice him—and he couldn't blame her—but Geoffrey noticed. He didn't stop moving, but he tilted his head and looked at Nash quizzically over the top of Sunny's head. Nash shook his head slightly. *I'm fine. I'll tell you later.*

And he would tell him. He was done keeping secrets, avoiding the situation, trying to stay away from sticky emotional situations. Geoffrey deserved better from him—the very least he deserved was to know the truth. That was the very least they all deserved.

Nash tightened his grip on both of them and turned his mind off, allowing his body to take complete control and turn itself over to the building pleasure and quickening tempo. Sunny flung her head back, her shouts dying as she struggled to breathe. Nash could sympathize. His throat was so tight, and with every thrust, fresh desire and pleasure exploded in him.

Nash didn't know who started moving faster, who initially reached for more. It could have been Sunny, impatient with the slow, careful rhythm they had established. It could have been Geoffrey, driven by the heat of her body to seek out more friction, more pressure. It could have been himself. But they all shifted, like they were being controlled by one mind, one purpose. In a way they were, Nash supposed.

"Sunny...Jesus Christ...Sunny...oh, Sunny..." Geoffrey panted, her name escaping his mouth on each breath. It joined her moans and Nash's harsh breathing to make a chorus, a song that wasn't quite tuneless and had a good tempo, a rhythm you could dance to.

"I want to feel you come, Geoffrey..." Sunny said, each word clearly coming at a great effort. "I want to feel you now, Geoff. Please."

Geoffrey tensed. "Oh, fuck."

Nash could feel Geoffrey's cock spasm deep inside of Sunny, jerking frantically against his own shaft. Sunny clenched, her entire body shuddering as her orgasm followed quickly on the heels of Geoffrey's. The combination of her hot muscles tensing around his cock, and the added friction of Geoffrey's jerking cock made Nash's eyes roll to the back of his head. He wanted the moment to last indefinitely, wanted the second to stretch so he could milk the experience for every last drop of pleasure.

Nash's orgasm started at the base of his spine, and before it erupted through him, he sought out Sunny's clit. It was swollen, still twitching from her climax, and he pinched it with just enough force to send her over the edge again. The quick, hot fluttering of her pussy around his cock was enough to send him into orbit, and his vision blurred as he came.

They came apart slowly, Geoffrey moving away first to discard the condom.

"I'm hungry again," Sunny murmured, collapsing against Nash's chest.

"There's still a sandwich or two."

Geoffrey stretched out on the bed and gently pulled Sunny against him, giving Nash a chance to stand and stretch his legs. He stood by the edge of the bed, studying the two of them as they curled around each other. His heart swelled, and he knew that his epiphany was true. He didn't know how to tell Geoffrey, but he knew he would. Before they returned to Los Angeles.

"Gonna lay down?" Geoff asked.

"I'm going to take a shower. You're welcome to join me. Both of you. It's big enough."

Sunny opened her eyes. "Really?"

"Yes."

"I could use a shower."

Nash held out his hand and helped her to her feet. "Geoffrey?"

"Who am I to say no?" Geoffrey asked, swinging his legs over the edge of the bed. "I think this suite also comes equipped with a hot tub."

Sunny's eyes lit up. "Maybe we should..."

"Shower first," Nash said. "Get rid of the sweat and the...other bodily fluids."

"I think you should get a hot tub installed, Geoff."

"Why me?"

"You're the only one in a house, not an apartment."

"She has a point," Nash agreed, herding them both toward the bathroom.

"I'll consider it," Geoffrey said.

"Please?"

Geoff eyed her. "You don't play fair, you know that?"

"Sure I do. I'm just asking. I could find other ways to...convince you. Now that would be playing dirty."

Nash closed the bathroom door behind them and grinned. "Let's see what dirty things you can do."

"That sounds like a challenge," Sunny said.

"More like a request," Nash said while Geoffrey reached into the stall and turned on the hot water.

"Oh, requests I can do. You know how I aim to please." She kissed him and stepped under the spray. "But first, who's going to wash my back?"

CHAPTER 15

Geoffrey took a deep breath, inhaling the salty air, and smiled. The bay was blue and smooth as glass, reflecting the cloudless sky above them. The sun was mellow and warm, and the breeze coming off the water was cool, but not cold. It was an unexpectedly perfect day in San Francisco, made even better by the company.

He looked over his shoulder and watched Nash and Sunny. They were sharing a beer and pointing across the water to the seals. Sunny was laughing at something Nash had said, and Nash was smiling, and Geoffrey still couldn't quite believe he was there. Couldn't quite believe he could go over and join them if he liked.

Nash looked up, grinned at him, then excused himself from Sunny and crossed the deck of the ferry to join him at the railing.

"I think we chose a good weekend to come up here," Nash said.

"Indeed."

"You want a beer?"

"No," Geoffrey turned back to the bay, "I'm good."

"We're going to need to do this again sometime soon," Nash said, "except for longer than a weekend."

Geoffrey nodded. "Yeah, but we've got to be careful."

"About what?"

"About getting work done."

Nash laughed. "Yeah, no kidding."

Geoffrey looked at him sideways. "That occurred to you, too?"

"Of course."

"I'm going to have to be the responsible one, aren't I?"

"You don't *have* to be responsible..."

Geoffrey snorted, and took a step closer to Nash, naturally seeking out any contact possible. "And I suppose we don't have to eat and pay rent."

"I promise, I'll behave myself."

"You know, I've heard that before. And it's never true."

Nash grinned. "But you love me anyway."

Geoffrey looked up, startled. That was the first time either of them mentioned the L word, or Geoffrey's emotions, since the subject first came up. Several times, he'd found himself wanting to blurt it out, especially when Nash was buried in his ass and everything seemed to be right there at the surface. But he didn't know if Nash wanted to hear it, or if he should say it, or if they were just going to pretend it wasn't there.

"Yeah," Geoffrey agreed softly. "I do."

"Geoffrey..."

"Yeah?"

"I wanted to..." He rubbed the back of his neck. "This is harder than I thought."

"What is?"

"Trying to find a way to tell you I love you, too."

"I think you just did."

Nash nodded. "Yeah."

Geoffrey covered Nash's hand with his own, and looked out over the water. He had been waiting for, hoping for, even praying for, those very words for years, and now he had them. Warmth spread through his chest, and he felt heavy, and light, and like shouting.

"I know that was a long time coming," Nash said softly.

"It was worth the wait," Geoffrey murmured.

"How do you feel?"

Geoffrey looked over his shoulder to Sunny, who still seemed entranced by the local wildlife. "I feel happy." She turned and looked at them then, and he beckoned her over. She hurried over and threw her arms around him, pulling him into a tight hug. "Really happy."

"Really happy about what?" Sunny asked.

"That we're all here and together," Geoffrey answered, "and in love."

Sunny looked from Geoffrey to Nash and her face broke out in a wide smile that rivaled the light from the sun. "Yeah. We are."

Geoffrey kissed the top of her head, then leaned over and brushed his lips across Nash's cheek.

"You know, we're never going to get any work done," Sunny said.

Geoffrey and Nash both laughed. "We'll figure something out," Nash promised her.

"We already did. I'm going to be the responsible one."

Sunny looked up, squinting in the sun. "Do you think you can resist both of us?"

Geoffrey smiled. "I know I can't. But then, I don't really want to."

"Then how can you be the responsible one?" Sunny asked.

"I guess we're all going to starve."

"What? We can't survive on love?" Nash asked.

"That's a myth," Geoffrey answered. "But I think we can find a way to balance our responsibilities with our…"

"Insane lust?" Sunny provided.

"I don't think I can resist my insane lust," Nash said. "Let's go back to the hotel."

"You mean after we see Alcatraz?" Geoffrey asked.

Nash smiled. "No, I mean now."

"You're insatiable."

"Alcatraz will be there tomorrow."

Geoffrey kissed him again. "Indeed, it will. What do you say, Sunny?"

"I say I need to get you two alone again."

Geoffrey nodded in agreement. They were both smiling and seemed to be shining in the sunlight, and his heart twisted. Of course the two of them belonged together. Anybody with eyes could see that. But now he was a part of them. It was nothing that Geoffrey could have foreseen, could have planned, or could even quite believe. He only knew that he needed them, and now he knew, they needed him as well.

He'd had no idea.

Of course they belonged together.

PEPPER ESPINOZA

Pepper Espinoza lives in southern California with her husband and her cats. She has spent the last year working as a full time author, and intends to start graduate school in the fall.

You can learn more about Pepper by visiting her website:

http://www.pepperverse.net

*   *   *

**Don't miss *The Streets of Florence*, by Pepper Espinoza,
available at AmberHeat.com!**

Anthony has spent his entire adult life chasing Christine, but she never allows herself to be caught. Once he finally stops searching for her, he runs into her on a business trip to Florence. He knows it can only end as it always does, with her walking out and him heartbroken. Nevertheless, he follows her back to her hotel, where he learns a shocking secret that can turn their entire relationship upside down...

AMBER QUILL PRESS, LLC
THE GOLD STANDARD IN PUBLISHING

QUALITY BOOKS
IN BOTH PRINT AND ELECTRONIC FORMATS

ACTION/ADVENTURE	SUSPENSE/THRILLER
SCIENCE FICTION	PARANORMAL
MAINSTREAM	MYSTERY
FANTASY	EROTICA
ROMANCE	HORROR
HISTORICAL	WESTERN
YOUNG ADULT	NON-FICTION

AMBER QUILL PRESS, LLC
http://www.amberquill.com

Made in the USA